# His grip was so w

Five years had passed since the last time he touched her. She'd known him for one week. And still, she'd never stopped missing him. Memories of their time together swirled in her head. She wanted to cry.

She wanted to scream.

"Just tell me." He gave her hand a squeeze. "It's okay. Just say it, whatever it is."

Now his touch burned her. "Please. You need to let go."

He released her. She yanked her hand back to her side of the table.

"Sorry," he said. "I didn't mean to—"

"It's okay. It's nothing you did. It's..." Payton blurted it out. "Easton, I, um, I had your babies."

The silence that followed seemed to go on forever.

Finally, a sound escaped him, something midway between a groan and a sigh. He sat back, hard, as though she'd shoved him in the chest. "What did you just say?"

She'd stopped breathing at some point and she had to make herself do that. Gulping in a giant breath of air, she nodded. "I got pregnant five years ago." She forced the truth out, fast. Frantic. "We have identical twins, boys, Penn and Bailey."

Dear Reader,

I'm so excited to share with you the first book in an all-new series. Wild Rose Sisters is a sweet, sexy trilogy starring three half sisters raised on a farm near the small imaginary town of Heartwood, Oregon. Less than an hour's drive east from Portland, Heartwood is right next door to the gorgeous real town of Hood River.

So welcome to Heartwood, where Payton Dahl, youngest of the sisters, has decided to make a few changes in her life. Always the fun one, full of life and eager for the next new experience, Payton has spent most of her life flitting from one temptation to the next. Men? Who can count on them? For love, good advice and support, she's always had the wonderful aunt who raised her and her two half sisters, Alex and Josie.

But flitting from one life experience to the next has grown less and less fulfilling lately. Payton has dreams she needs to fulfill. To that end, since last New Year's, she's put a lid on her active social life. For months now, nothing has distracted her from fulfilling her new goals. At least not until a dead boring night in October when a tall, hot stranger named Easton provides way more temptation than Payton can resist...

Like all my stories, *The Father of Her Sons* is about finding true love and keeping it, about the powerful connection between siblings, about the bonds we cherish with family and friends. I do hope you enjoy spending a little time in Heartwood with Payton and her sisters at Wild Rose Farm.

Happy reading, everyone!

*Christine*

# The Father
# of Her Sons

—

## CHRISTINE RIMMER

HARLEQUIN
SPECIAL
EDITION

ISBN-13: 978-1-335-40815-0

The Father of Her Sons

Copyright © 2021 by Christine Rimmer

This edition published by arrangement with Harlequin Books S.A.

For questions and comments about the quality of this book, please contact us at CustomerService@Harlequin.com.

Harlequin Enterprises ULC
22 Adelaide St. West, 40th Floor
Toronto, Ontario M5H 4E3, Canada
www.Harlequin.com

**Printed in U.S.A.**

**Christine Rimmer** came to her profession the long way around. She tried everything from acting to teaching to telephone sales. Now she's finally found work that suits her perfectly. She insists she never had a problem keeping a job—she was merely gaining "life experience" for her future as a novelist. Christine lives with her family in Oregon. Visit her at christinerimmer.com.

## Books by Christine Rimmer

### Harlequin Special Edition

#### *The Bravos of Valentine Bay*

*Almost a Bravo*
*Same Time, Next Christmas*
*Switched at Birth*
*A Husband She Couldn't Forget*
*The Right Reason to Marry*
*Their Secret Summer Family*
*Home for the Baby's Sake*
*A Temporary Christmas Arrangement*
*The Last One Home*

#### *Montana Mavericks: What Happened to Beatrix?*

*In Search of the Long-Lost Maverick*

#### *Montana Mavericks: Six Brides for Six Brothers*

*Her Favorite Maverick*

#### *Montana Mavericks: The Lonelyhearts Ranch*

*A Maverick to (Re)Marry*

Visit the Author Profile page at Harlequin.com for more titles.

For MSR, always.

## Chapter One

It all started with a little innocent flirting.

And okay, yes. Payton Dahl had given up flirting. Flirting too easily led to fooling around. Fooling around often became romance and right now in her life, she had no time at all for romantic entanglements—not even brief ones, which were pretty much the only kind she'd ever known. She spent her nights tending bar and her days either helping at the family farm or huddled over her laptop.

For more than nine months, from January well into October, Payton had stuck with her plan to avoid men altogether. Yes, she'd been tempted more than once by a sexy smile or a smoldering pair of bedroom eyes. She'd kept her eyes on the prize, though. She'd said no to temptation. Payton had stories inside her head. She intended to get them written down. That required discipline and for months, she'd exercised strict self-control.

But then, on a Wednesday night in mid-October,

a whole new level of temptation came calling, one that had *irresistible* written all over him.

That particular Wednesday night, the Larch Tree Lounge at the Heartwood Inn was deader than a frozen doorknob. In one of the booths, a very tired looking middle-aged couple argued in whispers without much enthusiasm. Cletus Carnigan, a nightly fixture in the lounge, sat slumped at one end of the bar gazing mournfully into his Logsdon Lager.

As usual, it promised to be a very long night—until a tall, broad-shouldered stranger with tousled dark blond hair and cheekbones sharp as knives in his stunning, angular face took the stool at the opposite end of the bar from Cletus.

*No flirting*, Payton sternly reminded herself. Pasting on her most professional smile, she marched down the bar to greet the smoking-hot newcomer. "Welcome to the Larch Tree Lounge. What can I get you?"

He ordered Redbreast Irish Whiskey, an admirable choice—both good quality and excellent value for the money. "And something to eat," he added. "What's good?"

"Right off the bat with the loaded question," she muttered under her breath.

He narrowed his gorgeous blue eyes at her. "Is there a problem?"

"Sort of." Unfortunately, not much was good

at the Larch Tree Lounge. And while Payton despised lying to her customers, telling a guest that the food sucked wouldn't do, either. She settled for evasion. "What are you in the mood for?"

He studied her face at length. She stared right back at him for way too long while hummingbirds flitted around in her belly and an electric current went snapping and popping beneath the surface of her skin. Finally, he folded his lean hands on the bar, canted toward her and spoke confidentially. "It's all bad. Is that what you're telling me?"

So much for evasion. What now? She didn't want to lie about the food, but she didn't want to get fired, either. Her best option at this point? Maybe a recommendation. The burgers were passable. "How about a burger?"

He was hiding a grin. She could see it kind of pulling at one corner of that fine mouth of his. "An honest woman."

Not exactly. An honest woman would admit that the food sucked. She plucked a menu from the stand on her side of the bar and held it out to him. "Need a minute to decide?"

He let out a chuckle heavily laced with irony. "The burger's fine. Fries?"

"Will do." She propped the menu in the stand again.

"Wait," he said, before she could turn for the

kitchen. "Why do I get the feeling you're going to cook my dinner?"

"Because I am."

"A multitasker, huh?"

She gave him a modest little smile as she swept out a hand to include the couple in the booth and Cletus staring into his beer. "As you can see, it's a slow night. On slow nights, the cook goes home at seven—but don't worry. I know how to work the grill and the deep fryer." She shouldn't wink at him. Winking was straight-up flirting. No excuse for it.

She did it, anyway.

"Thank you." He raised his whiskey glass to her, his gaze shifting for half a second to the name tag pinned above her left breast. "Payton."

"My pleasure."

In the kitchen, Payton found the inn's manager, Midge Shanahan, lurking on the far side of the narrow doorway from the bar, like a spider in her web.

Midge said nothing at first. Payton breezed by her, washed her hands, took a patty from the fridge and dropped it on the grill. She tossed a generous serving of fries into the fryer basket and set up a burger plate. As Payton worked, Midge crossed her skinny arms over her narrow chest and kept quiet.

Unfortunately, Midge Shanahan never stayed quiet for long.

"You are not paid to get cozy with the customers." Midge spoke the words in a near whisper, heavy on the venom. "I saw you out there just now." Payton gave Mr. Hottie an extra slice of tomato, then granted Midge a nod and a cool smile. "What?" demanded Midge. "Cat got that smart tongue of yours?"

The first few times Midge had started in on her for no reason, Payton had played it sweet, bewildered and innocent—because she really had done nothing wrong. For a while after that, she'd tried defending herself. Once she'd even threatened to quit. But she hadn't quit. And in time she'd figured out that Midge had no plans to fire her. Midge Shanahan was just a wall of ugly sound. She never took action to back up the vitriol.

Nowadays, when Midge jumped her ass, Payton only smiled politely and went on working. She'd learned over time that Midge gave up the attack more quickly if she got no pushback.

"It's very quiet tonight," Midge remarked after a lovely thirty seconds of silence.

"Yes, it is." Payton flipped Hottie's burger.

"You think you can manage the lounge without me?" Midge asked in a grudging tone. She was supposed to pinch-hit as the cook if things picked up later in the evening. That rarely happened, though, and almost never on a weeknight. As a rule, Tuesday through Thursday, around 8:00 p.m., Midge would disappear into her little apartment off the lobby and only emerge again if someone rang the bell out front in search of a room.

"Of course I can manage, Midge."

"Well." Midge gave a small, disdainful sniff, as though she smelled something bad. "All right, then. I'll see you tomorrow night."

Yes, she would. Unfortunately. Payton worked Tuesday through Saturday. "Night, Midge." She lowered the fry basket into the fryer as Midge disappeared through the door that led to the lobby.

Back in the lounge a few minutes later, Payton served the blue-eyed hottie his burger and poured him a second Irish whiskey. The weary couple left.

Cletus drank his beer in one long gulp and plunked it down. "Payton. 'Nother, please."

She served him, cleaned up after the couple and tackled some side work that would need doing before she left at the end of the night.

Mr. Hottie finished his burger. She cleared off his plate for him, taking special care not to meet his eyes. Those eyes lured her to places she'd sworn not to go—at least not until she'd completed the final book in her epic fantasy series.

"Payton?" That voice. She felt it like a quick brush of rough velvet across her skin.

Against her better judgment, she looked up from the bar towel in her hand and straight into those dangerous eyes. "Hmm?"

"Were you *trying* not to look at me?"

She gave it up with a shrug. "Yeah."

"Why?"

"Does it matter? I'm looking at you now."

His gaze shifted—from her eyes to her mouth and back to her eyes again. "You are so incredibly appealing."

What a line the guy had. She shouldn't believe him. She *didn't* believe him. But she felt flattered all the same. Any guy might call her beautiful when making his move. But *appealing*. It had a sweet note of sincerity to it, as though he'd sat there and thought about it before choosing that word specifically for her.

And there was more. He added, as though reading her mind, "I shouldn't be flirting with you."

She had to stifle a chuckle. "No, you should not."

"But I can't seem to stop myself. You should probably just ignore me."

She hummed low in her throat again. "I *was* ignoring you—or trying to, anyway."

"Why?"

"Let's just say I have big plans and they don't include getting sidetracked by a man."

Oh, the way he looked at her. Like he wanted to eat her right up. "Plans like what?"

"Plans like finishing my blockbuster fantasy trilogy."

"You're a writer." He said it without a trace of irony—and that made him all the more attractive to her. As rule, she never mentioned her writing goals to customers at the lounge. Why set herself up for derision? Nobody wanted to hear about the bartender's big dreams. They wanted fast service, a friendly smile and a sympathetic ear when they were feeling down.

She gave him a firm nod. "I am a writer, yes— or at least I am when I'm not serving drinks, flipping burgers or pitching in at the family farm..."

"A very busy writer is what you're saying."

"That is exactly what I'm saying."

"I get that. And I have no intention of sidetracking you in any way."

She frowned at him. "I have two questions."

"Ask them."

"First name?"

"Easton."

She liked his name. It had a manly, straightforward, both-feet-on-the-ground sound to it. "So, Easton, are you married?"

He didn't look away when she asked that one. She considered that a good sign. "I'm divorced. Very recently divorced. I got the final papers a few days ago."

"My condolences."

"Thank you." He took a slow sip of his whiskey. "It's an old story. We were college sweethearts. We grew apart. It took a few years, but we finally had to accept that we wanted different things. And how about you, Payton—married or otherwise committed?"

"Nope. On both counts."

The outer door opened, ushering in a gust of cold October air along with two women Payton had never seen before. They took the booth the weary couple had vacated.

"Excuse me," she said, and went to wait on them.

The two women ordered cosmos, mozzarella sticks and artichoke dip. Payton gave them their drinks, prepared their snacks and served them. The whole time she felt edgy, her skin prickly with reluctant awareness. She tried not to glance Easton's way, but then did it, anyway. Twice. Both times, he was watching her. And both times he grinned, a wry twist of those gorgeous lips, as if to say, *What can I tell you? I like looking at you…*

"Another whiskey?" she asked him after she'd left the two ladies munching mozzarella sticks, enjoying their drinks.

"Better not." He asked for the check, added a huge tip, charged it to room 203 and scrawled an illegible signature.

"Thank you," she said sincerely. Huge tips were few and far between in the lounge.

"You're welcome."

Down the bar, Cletus sighed dramatically. He was a sweet guy whose wife had left him recently. She went on down to him. "You doing okay, Cletus?"

"'Nother?" He glanced up at her hopefully. When she held her ground and crossed her arms, he let out another hard sigh. "I been here four hours, had four drinks. A man's body can process one drink per hour. And I am not driving, Payton. Fergus is picking me up at midnight." Fergus was his older brother. She felt a warm tug of relief that the family was looking out for him.

"It's your liver." She poured him another one—after which she tried her best not to wander back on down the bar to the irresistible, just-divorced man she needed to avoid more contact with. Why didn't he leave? He'd paid his bill. She'd cleared the bar in front of him.

He sent her a glance at the same time as she just happened to look his way.

And that did it. Her resistance simply melted. She liked him. When he looked at her, she felt energized. Inspired. Like a story that begged to be written, he called to her without saying a word.

She zipped down the bar so fast, she was lucky

the memory-foam soles of her clunky work shoes didn't catch fire.

"I think I need one more whiskey." He rubbed his sculpted jaw in a rueful way. "Otherwise, I'll have no excuse not to head on back to my room…"

She gave him his drink. They started talking. He said he was in town on business. Payton pondered that. Heartwood was a farming community. Was he thinking of buying a farm? Before she could ask, he said, "It's beautiful here," scanning her face as he spoke, wearing a look that said *she* was beautiful.

She thought about how long it had been since she'd felt like this, light as a ball of cottonwood fluff blown on a summer breeze.

Yeah. Way too long. Maybe never—not *quite* like this, anyway.

"What?" he asked softly.

Before she could decide whether or not to confess that he pushed all her buttons in the best kind of way, one of the cosmo drinkers signaled for another round and three guys who worked construction for a local builder came in.

As Payton mixed drinks and whipped out sliders and sweet potato fries, she thought how she *shouldn't*. She couldn't. She wouldn't. She really, really should not be thinking what she was thinking.

But Easton rang all her bells—rang them so

loud she could think of nothing else but how sweet it might be to spend a little private time with him.

And didn't she deserve a bit of fun now and then? She'd spent the last nine and a half months driving herself without letup, slogging staunchly through each dead boring night here, putting in her time on the farm in the mornings and then, finally, working the main goal—to get words on the page. Since January, she'd kept her focus strictly on what mattered, pouring all her energy into her own personal dream of making a living from the stories that filled her head.

*It's just, he's so hot*, wheedled her internal teenager. *He's hot and he likes me and I like him so much!*

She knew she was in really big trouble when she started mentally agreeing with that teenager, aka her weaker self—the one who loved a good time more than she should, the one who still longed to stay up all night playing guitar and singing backup for the Millhouse Madmen, four guys she'd grown up with who came home now and then from Portland, where they waited tables for a living and occasionally snared a gig as a cover band.

*He's so pretty*, whined the party girl within. *It could be perfect. No strings. One night, that's all. No more, I promise…*

Fergus showed up and Cletus reluctantly followed him out. The two women went home and the construction guys asked for the check.

By one, the place had emptied out. Just Payton and Easton, easy conversation and a heaping helping of delicious sexual tension. They talked and laughed uninterrupted for the next forty-five minutes.

Easton said he worked for his family's company, but he never said the name of that company or what the company did—and she didn't ask. It became like a game, with both of them taking care to give away no details of their separate lives. They joked about it, agreed that they didn't need last names or unnecessary details. They were enjoying each other's company on a dreary October night and that was enough for both of them.

As closing time approached, he said, "Payton, I can't remember when I've had such a good time."

*Oh, me neither!* she squealed internally. She felt so good, like a little girl again, about seven years old with a giant bag of Skittles she didn't have to share with her sisters. She laughed. "No better way to spend your Wednesday night than chatting up the bartender at the Larch Tree Lounge."

"That's right—as long as the bartender is you." He stared in her eyes and then he shifted his gaze downward to her mouth. And then he did it all over again, that focused stare going back and forth—her eyes, her mouth, her eyes, her mouth…

Her lips kind of tingled. They'd been doing that a lot the past few hours, making her want to rub them, making her wonder what it might be like to kiss him—wondering that had slowly turned to yearning and, in the past hour or so, started feeling something like obsession.

She longed to kiss him. She could almost feel the press of his lips to hers. She wanted it so bad.

"Yeah." She sounded breathless and she didn't even care that he had to know he'd made her that way. "The hours crawl by around here, as a rule. Not tonight, though."

And then, that burning gaze on her mouth again, he said what they were both thinking. "I wish it didn't have to end."

Oh, yeah. There it was. The invitation. It hung in the air between them, a question phrased as a statement.

*Let it go. Just agree with him. You had your fun, indulged yourself in some lovely flirting with a hot side of teasing. Now be a good girl like you promised you would and tell the man good-night...*

He waited. Their eyes held. Neither of them seemed to be breathing.

She felt she hovered on the edge of a dangerous cliff.

And then she surrendered. She let herself fall. "If you'll give me fifteen minutes, it doesn't have to end."

## Chapter Two

When Payton emerged from the side door, she spotted Easton immediately. In the hard, white glare of the tall parking lot lights, his hair gleamed a rich gold color and his eyes looked shadowed, full of hidden intent, as he leaned against the back of a low black sports car. Definitely a guy exciting enough to have her throwing her jealously guarded discipline to the wind—if only for one night.

She shivered in the icy air and drew her puffy jacket tighter around her. "Nice car."

He gave her a lazy shrug. "It's a rental."

She felt awkward, suddenly. And terribly unsure in her ugly work shoes, cheap jeans and worn jacket. "I would invite you to my place. I have my own little house. But mine's not the only house on our farm. I also have a mama-bear older sister living in the house next door to mine. Across a stretch of grass, there's an aunt I adore who would ask a million questions. I don't need the questions—I really don't."

"So they're judgmental, your sister and your aunt?"

"Not in the least. But they love me and they're not shy about asking me personal questions. I don't want to deal with any of that, you know?" *I just want this one night, a break from my own rules and plans.* Was that so much to ask?

He looked at her with absolute focus, not once glancing away. "Come up to my room."

She laughed, a nervous sound. "Also, there's Midge."

"The manager, you mean?"

She nodded. "Joining a guest in his room is a major no-no. If Midge catches me with you, she'll get me fired and she'll be justified in doing it."

Would Midge actually follow through? Payton couldn't be certain. So far, Midge had not once followed through on even one of her never-ending threats. But Payton had a really strong feeling that sleeping with a visitor would do the trick. If Midge found out she'd gone upstairs with Easton, Payton would never work another shift behind the bar in the Larch Tree Lounge.

The thought almost had her grinning. Really, would that be such a bad thing? No more tedious nights babysitting Cletus, washing dishes and frying burgers between way-too-occasional customers?

Yes, she reminded herself. It *would* be a bad

thing. Jobs in Heartwood didn't grow on trees—especially not jobs that fit perfectly into the tight schedule she'd set for herself. Plus, Easton *was* a guest and that made sleeping with him unethical.

Payton's wild side, too long suppressed, cried out, *Do it! Please! So what if you lose your tacky bartending gig? He's so hot and hunky!*

Easton tipped his head to the side, his gaze never wavering. "Let's go somewhere else, then."

This time her laugh was more of a scoff. "It's Heartwood. Last-minute lodging alternatives are thin on the ground around here. We might get a room with a really uncomfortable box-spring bed at the motel right off the highway. Wouldn't that be fun?"

He peeled his long, strong frame off the back of the car and closed the distance between them. Her body vibrated with pure physical longing at his nearness. Their breath misted in the air between them. He reached out. She held his gaze *and* her ground.

And the most wonderful thing happened.

For the first time, he touched her.

Taking hold of her puffy collar with both hands, he tucked it closer around her against the early-morning chill. The back of his thumbs brushed the sides of her neck, sending a cascade of shivers flowing over her skin.

In a whisper, he asked, "Are you changing your mind about this?"

"Are you kidding? And miss the chance to pull one over on Midge?" She bit the corner of her lip and he watched her do it, his own lips softly parting, as though her slightest action fascinated him. "No, Easton," she added to make herself perfectly clear. "I'm not changing my mind."

"Good." He leaned in. She felt his lips on hers—just a light brush of a touch. Barely a touch at all, really.

Yet it echoed through her, sweet and thrilling, heavy with the promise of what was to come.

"I was thinking you would go up first." She looked at him from under her lashes, feeling sheepish. She'd always been the bold one, up for anything, willing to own her choices, however unwise. And yet, to keep this crappy job, she would lower herself to sneaking around—correction. She would sneak around in order to get one night with Easton *and* keep this crappy job. "I'm going to move my pickup out of the lot. I'll be up in ten minutes, tops."

"I'll be waiting." He kissed her again, a little more slowly. She yearned for the next kiss. And the one after that.

And really, why hadn't she just stayed on the pill when she swore off men? Shouldn't she have anticipated that at some point, a guy she couldn't resist would come along? "You have condoms?"

"I do."

"Okay, then. Ten minutes."

"It's room—"

"203. I remember. Go to your room, Easton. Get ready for me to rock your world."

The Heartwood Inn website and brochures touted the place as a resort. In truth, it was more of a glorified motel created by adding a couple of ugly extensions onto a huge, rambling log home. The gorgeous wooded setting didn't hurt, though.

And as luck would have it, 203 was a suite in one of the added-on wings accessed along an out-side hall. Yes, she had a master key, but sneaking in through the lobby would have posed quite the challenge, Midge-wise. The woman had X-ray vision and sensitive ears.

The door to 203 swung open before she could knock. Easton's slow smile caused havoc in her belly. "You came."

Her heart thudded so hard that the sound pulsed in her ears. "Not yet, but I hope so."

He took her hand and pulled her over the threshold into the knotty-pine splendor within. The door swung shut.

She took in the sitting area complete with a work desk and a large open laptop with a screensaver of the Cape Disappointment lighthouse. A cheery gas fire burned in the rustic natural stone fireplace. The king-size bed across the room was crafted of twisting aspen logs. "I hear the beds are comfortable."

"Yes, they are."

"Too bad about all the plaid." Every inch of fabric in the room—curtains, comforter, pillows and upholstery—all of it was red-and-green plaid.

His eyes stayed locked on her. "Yeah. Among other things, the decor could use some work— God, you are gorgeous." He drew in a slow breath. "And you smell like—"

"Beer and sweet potato fries?"

"Shut up." He circled her throat with his big hand. She sighed at the contact as he tipped her face higher and took her mouth.

Kiss number three at last—and oh my goodness, the man knew what to do with those fine lips of his. If she did get fired for this, at least it promised to be a night to remember.

When she opened her eyes again, he was watching her. Lost in the moment, she gazed right back at him. Anticipation thrummed along every nerve she possessed as he unzipped her jacket and slid it off her shoulders, dropping it and her cross-body bag on a chair. Next, he took her Larch Tree Lounge T-shirt by the hem and tugged it upward.

When she lifted her arms, he whipped it off and tossed it away.

He kissed her again. Their tongues tangled and danced as he unbuttoned her jeans and pushed at them, taking her panties along for the ride.

That time, when he released her mouth, she looked down between them at the wad of denim and cotton stuck at her knees. "Getting undressed is so awkward sometimes."

He tipped up her chin with a finger. "I'm willing to help."

"I noticed. I like that about you—I like a lot of things about you."

"Tell me more." He scooped her up in his arms and carried her to the turned-back bed.

"Hmm. The way you kiss, those blue, blue eyes…"

Setting her gently down, he removed her shoes and socks. A moment later, he tossed her jeans and panties over his shoulder. Naked except for her plain white sports bra, she gazed up at him looming above her.

"Now, your hair," he said, his voice skirting close to reverence. "Come closer." She scooted toward him to the edge of the bed. His fingers swift and adept, he pulled out the pins that anchored the brown waves in a sloppy bun. Released, her hair fell to her shoulders. Setting the pins on the bedside table next to a mound of condoms, he combed his fingers through the strands. "There." He backed off a little and just looked at her. "Perfect." He seemed completely sincere.

And she still had on her utterly unsexy bra. Swiftly, she wiggled out of it. Hooking it on one of the twisted aspen branches that made up the headboard, she dropped flat on her back across the mattress.

Looking mesmerized, he watched her every move. "You're like no woman I've ever met before."

She sat up again and scooted back to his side of the bed. Going to her knees, she began unbuttoning his soft wool shirt. "How so?"

"You're so comfortable inside your own skin. Does anything ever intimidate you?"

"Not really." She undid the last button. "And I like you, too, Easton. A lot."

He took off the shirt and dropped it to the rug.

"You're so..." She ran appreciative hands over the lean, muscular terrain of his chest.

"I'm so what?" He gave her a teasing smile.

"Words fail me. That doesn't happen often." He felt so good, both silky and hard. The trail of light brown hair that ran across his pecs and down the middle of his torso felt crisp and inviting to her touch.

She met his eyes again. It would be quite the challenge to walk away from him—but she would do it, she promised herself.

He wrapped those hard arms around her. She sighed into the next kiss, her fingers busy at his fly…

Four a.m. came much too soon.

"I have to get home," she said lazily.

He lifted up from his pillow and leaned close. "Stay." Then he kissed her.

The thing was, she wanted to stay. She wanted to stay really bad. But she had to get out well before daylight or risk the wrath of Midge. "Can't. Sorry." Easing free of his hold, she pushed back the covers.

He braced up on an elbow and watched her walk around the bed, gathering up her clothes as she went. "Payton."

She wriggled into her bra. "Hmm?"

"I'm here for the next week. I want to see you again."

She pulled on her plain white granny panties, put on her T-shirt and shimmied into her jeans.

When she perched on the edge of the bed to put on her socks and shoes, he sat up and moved in closer behind her. She felt his touch on her neck, the warm pads of his fingers guiding her hair to the side. Her breath got stuck in her throat as he pressed those plush, adept lips to the crook of her neck.

A tiny groan just might have escaped her. "Easton…"

"Are you working tonight?" His voice caressed her, a soft growl, so tender—and so very insistent. He scraped his teeth across her skin.

Every molecule in her body moaned in pleasure.

She shouldn't encourage him, but how could she help it? With an audible sigh, she sagged back against him.

He took her earlobe between his teeth and worried it gently. "Answer me."

"Fine. Yeah. I'm working tonight."

"What time?"

"Six to closing."

"I'll see you then." He licked the spot he'd bitten a moment ago and her brain fogged over with lust.

*Pull it together, Payton.* She needed to remind him that this had only been for tonight.

But he'd said he would be here for a week…

A week, and then he would go back to wherever he came from.

She did want to see him again. And really, why shouldn't she at least consider spending some time with him while he was in town? After all, she'd been so very good for so damn long. She deserved a reward for her months of unremitting focus on her goals—a reward in the form of a little more quality time with this amazing man.

A week. A definite deadline, she thought as she put on her shoes. A week and then he would leave and she would get back to reality with renewed dedication, reenergized from a generous infusion of hot, sexy times.

Fully dressed now, she rose and turned to face him—and her midsection melted. He looked so good. His hair all scrambled up, his pillowy mouth now set in a determined line, with that glint in his eye that said he wasn't through with her yet.

And who did she think she was kidding? She wasn't through with him, either.

Walking backward, her gaze locked with his, she moved to the middle of the room to give herself much-needed distance from all that manliness. "We would have to set a few boundaries."

His gold-kissed eyebrows drew together. "What kind of boundaries?"

"Serious ones."

"Specifically?"

"Well, the problem is I really like you. So much."

"Payton. That is not a problem."

"Yes, it is. Because if we spend more time together, odds are I will only like you more. Boundaries would keep me from trying to get in touch with you in the future."

He gave her a level-eyed stare. "You do realize you don't even know my last name?"

"That's right. And you don't know mine and you're never going to."

"Whoa." His face fell as he fisted a hand and tapped it twice over his heart. "Hit me where it hurts, why don't you?"

"I'm sorry. I truly am. It's just… I dropped out of college, okay? Until recently, I never finished anything I started. I'm the fun one, the one who's easily distracted by the next shiny object. I love life and partying, playing music all night. But I've finally managed, for several months now, to buckle down and get to work making my dream of writing for a living come true. I have been staying on task, keeping my eye on my goals, doing what I need to do to make my dream real."

He watched her with such absolute focus. "That's good. That's great. And I'm not going to mess with your program—or if I do, I'll only mess with it a little. I just want to be with you whenever you have time while I'm in town."

"Yeah, but that's the thing. Yes, I want to see you again, but I really don't have any extra time."

His face hardened. "Make time."

She straightened her shoulders. "You know, the more I think about it, I really can't."

"You can. Look at it this way. You've been driving yourself nonstop for too long. You *need* a break. And I'm the one to give you what you need. You should be glad I showed up tonight."

She chuckled, shaking her head. His words so closely echoed what she'd been thinking. "You're very persistent."

He kept pushing. "I'm only here for a week. And then I'm gone. If you don't want to see me again after that, you won't. You have my word."

She stared at him, wanting exactly what he was offering her, and ridiculously glad that he wanted it, too. "I meant what I said, about the boundaries."

He didn't miss a beat. "Name them."

She stuck her hands in her pockets and stared down at the rug. "Okay. It would have to be no last names, no phone numbers, no email addresses. I don't want to know what you do or where you live. We can talk about our lives and our dreams and all that stuff in a general way, but no details. Nothing that would help us find each other later."

He shook his head and accused gruffly, "You want us to lie to each other?"

"What did I just say? Truth, about what we feel and what we want and what's happened to us in our separate lives. But no specifics, nothing that would help us keep in touch at the end of your stay here."

He swung his powerful legs over the edge of the bed. Sitting there, looking magnificent without a stitch on, he said, "We don't need these rules of yours."

"Think about it, Easton. Are you ready for your next relationship?"

"Payton, come on..."

"Please answer me. Are you?"

"No, but I—"

"I'm not ready, either. I've got stuff to do, and I can't be distracted by a guy—not even one as amazing as you are. I can't be tempted to grab my cell and ping you, to drop you a text, look you up on Facebook or Insta to see how you're doing, and then not be able to stop myself from getting in touch with you, from asking you oh so casually when maybe you might be thinking of returning to town."

He stared at her, his eyes shadowed. She could feel his reluctance to agree to her terms—at the same time as he knew he needed those terms, too.

She continued, "But this." She pointed at him and then back at herself. "This...chemistry. This thing we have, this energy between us? I want some more of it—I do. But I can only agree to more if we limit it to this one week."

His expression had lost that hard edge. Now he held her gaze in that tender way of his. "Just while I'm in town..."

"Yes. And then you go back to your life and I stay here in mine. We can't call. We can't write. We won't stay in touch no matter how strongly we might be tempted to because we'll have no way to reach out to each other."

He stood. "Payton."

So. Much. Man. She looked him up and down, longing to close the distance between them and throw herself against him, feel his arms come around her, breathe in the intoxicating scent of his skin, rip off her clothes all over again and pull him back down to the tangled sheets of his bed.

But she stayed where she was. "If you think it's too crazy and you don't want to do it, just say so." She turned to grab her jacket and purse off the chair by the door.

And suddenly he was right behind her. "Payton..." He took hold of her shoulders and pulled her to him, her back to his bare front. Those hard, hot arms went around her.

She felt herself weakening, sinking into his embrace.

He bent close and tucked his head in the crook of her neck. "You're right," he whispered. "I've been divorced for five minutes. I don't live nearby. I'll be finished here in a week and who knows where I'll be going next?"

She turned her head back to meet his eyes. He kissed her, a chaste kiss, but one that lingered.

When the kiss broke, she stepped free of his hold to face him again. "You know where I'll be tonight. You can think about it."

He laughed, a wry sound. "I'm in." Raking his scrambled hair back from his forehead with both hands, he said, "I'll see you tonight."

Her chest felt tight—a bittersweet ache. "We'll still need to watch out for Midge. Tending bar at the lounge is not a great job, but it works for me right now. I don't want to get fired."

He stepped close again and guided a hank of hair back behind the curve of her ear. "I understand."

"Come in after nine. Midge will be off for the night by then—or she should be. However, if by some miracle it's a busy night, she'll be at the grill in back..."

"I get it. If she's there, I won't stay. I'll come back here to my room and wait for you." They stared at each other. A thread of heat and yearning stretched between them, pulling them in.

She sucked in a hard breath. "Easton, I really do need to go."

"I know. Let me get dressed. I'll walk you to your—"

"No. There's no point. I'm out of here."

"One more kiss."

"Easton, I have to..."

But then he took her face between his hands. She surrendered to the magic of his mouth on hers.

In the end, with great reluctance, she made herself jerk away. "I need to go."

He put up both hands. "Got it." Stepping around her, he grabbed her coat and held it up for her. "Until tonight," he said as he helped her into it and handed her the purse. Turning, he pulled open the door. The wind blew in, cold. Bracing. She walked out fast, before she could weaken again and manufacture a reason to stay.

Thursday night at the lounge was slower than Wednesday.

Midge checked out at eight and Easton walked through the doors at nine on the nose. Payton's heart bounced around inside her chest just at the sight of him, in black jeans, a fisherman's sweater and soft tan boots. He hung his jacket by the door and took the same seat at the bar as the night before.

Payton served him nachos and a Wanderlust IPA, and they played it careful, chatting only a little as the hours ticked by, in case Cletus or one of the other five customers that evening just happened to be paying attention. It was unlikely, but you never knew. Some nosy regular might mention to Midge that the night bartender seemed to really like that good-looking guy from out of town.

Easton stuck around after he finished the nachos and beer. Payton felt a little guilty about that. He had to be as bored with the place as

she was. Strangely, though, with him there, the
lounge seemed so much less grim. She had something wonderful to look forward to after closing.
Easton's very presence had her feeling energized,
wearing a big, fat, happy smile.

Cletus even noticed her improved attitude,
though as a rule he rarely seemed to register anything but the beer in front of him and his own
current misery.

"Payton," he muttered when she set his fourth
beer on the bar for him.

"Yes, Cletus?"

He squinted at her and asked in an accusing
tone, "What're you smiling about?"

She consciously did not cast a dewy-eyed glance
down the bar at the broad-shouldered guy in the
fisherman's sweater. "Just feeling good, I guess."

"Well." He took a sip of his beer. "Chillax with
the perkiness. Life ain't that great."

She laughed. "Cletus, you are a ray of pure
sunshine."

"Knock it off," he grumbled as he slid off his
stool. "I'll be back. Don't touch my beer."

"Wouldn't dream of it."

He mumbled something she couldn't make out
as he headed for the men's room.

Cletus left with his brother at a little after eleven.

For the next two hours, it was just Payton and
Easton. They kept the talk casual—music pref-

erences, favorite movies, bucket-list travel destinations.

Being there all alone with him gave her ideas. Her wild side tried to mess with her. She kept fantasizing about getting frisky in one of the plaid-upholstered knotty-pine booths or maybe back in the kitchen or a stall in the ladies' room.

He picked up her dangerous vibe. "What? Tell me."

"This is not a good idea."

He scowled at that and then asked very carefully, "To what, exactly, are you referring?"

She answered quietly, though they were alone in the empty bar, "We need a new rule."

He swore under his breath. "We have enough rules."

"You can't hang around here all through my shift."

"I didn't get here till nine, as per your instructions."

"Ooo. *'As per.'* Fancy. Did you go to Yale?"

"No personal details." His voice was low, gravelly. She could feel it like a rough caress, rubbing her most sensitive places. "*Your* rule, remember—and why shouldn't I hang around here? I'm staying at the inn, I ordered food and a drink. If anyone has a right to take up a barstool in the Larch Tree Lounge and chat up the smoking-hot bartender, I think that would be me."

"Smoking-hot, am I?" She didn't know whether to laugh like a maniac, moan in sexual frustration—or simply leap across the bar and plaster her mouth to his.

"You know damn well you are." Slowly, he stood from the stool. She saw in his eyes what he would do and knew she should sternly remind him that he'd better not.

But all of a sudden, she had no words. She only stared at him, her lips softly parted, her breath coming shallow and fast.

He reached for her. Hooking his hand around the back of her neck, he dragged her toward him across the bar.

Their lips met. Her mind went deliciously blank and her body caught fire.

## Chapter Three

Heaven.

Easton's kiss burned through her, hot, hard and so, so good. She grabbed for him and he yanked her closer. Her feet left the floor mat. Menus and condiments tumbled to the floor.

She found herself laid out on the bar with him on top of her. His tongue was halfway down her throat and she just wanted it deeper. Slipping a big hand up under her shirt, he palmed her breast through the barrier of her bra—a nicer one than last night, one she'd put on expressly because he would be seeing it.

And as for her, flat on her back on the bar? The thing was, she loved it.

She didn't want it to stop. She wanted him to rip open her zipper, yank down her pants and get busy with her right then and there.

Yet somehow, in some tiny section of her sex-addled brain, she managed to hold on to a small, frayed thread of sanity.

Instead of clutching his big shoulders, pulling

him tighter, closer to her, she made herself shove at him, just hard enough to create a slight gap between his mouth and hers. "Stop," she panted, in barely more than a whisper.

He blinked down at her, his gorgeous face flushed, his full lips swollen, those hot-ice eyes burning right through her. "Payton, I'm sorry. I never…"

She silenced him with two fingertips against his mouth. "Stop. Get off me, please."

With a hard sigh, he pressed his forehead to hers. "Okay." Carefully, he climbed off the bar on his side as she slid to the mat on her side once again.

Straightening her bra with a quick tug on either side and pulling the hem of her T-shirt back down where it belonged, she cast a frantic glance at the row of windows that flanked the outside door. Nobody there—not anyone she could see, anyway. Not a sound from the kitchen.

She stared him squarely in the eye. "You need to leave. Please."

"But I'll see you at—"

She showed him the hand. "I'll be there. Go."

He stared down at her, not budging, a mutinous look in his eye. She feared he would actually refuse to leave.

But then, with a hard huff of breath and a shake of his head, he turned and started walking. Grabbing his spendy-looking jacket from the coat tree by the door, he went out. She watched him march past the windows, his thick hair gleaming beneath the row of lights that ran along the front of the building, quickly disappearing on his way to the stairs leading up to his suite.

She missed him already, the jerk.

Nobody else came in that night. She spent the remainder of her shift cleaning everything in sight, with extra emphasis on the bar itself. Once she'd closed up, she spent a few minutes primping in the ladies' room, taking her hair from its knot on top of her head, brushing it out, applying lip gloss and blusher like some anxious teenager anticipating her first date.

At twenty after two, Payton mounted the steps to the east wing. Just like last night, Easton pulled open the door as she raised her hand to knock.

"Thank God," he said, stepping back for her to enter. "I was afraid you wouldn't show." He shut the door and turned the lock as soon as she crossed the threshold.

She dropped her jacket and shoulder bag on the chair by the door and faced him. "I won't say I didn't love what happened before you left, but we both know it was out of control—not to mention inappropriate in the extreme." *Inappropriate*. She almost laughed. That was a word she'd never given a thought to until the past year, when she'd decided to rein in her inner party girl and nail down her goals.

Easton actually hung his head, like a small boy who'd been very bad and truly felt sorry for it. She wanted to step close, enfold him in her arms, muss up his hair and whisper words of understanding. As far as she knew, no one had witnessed their indiscretion. "No harm done."

He met her eyes. "Yeah?"

"Yeah. It's fine—I promise you."

He held out his hand. When she took it, he pulled her over to the bed. They sat on the edge, side by side. "I never do crap like that." He slid her a glance. "I'm the nice brother."

She gave his hand a squeeze. "You have a brother?"

"What? It's against the rules to mention a brother?"

"Hmm. Well, that wouldn't be fair."

"Right. You told me you have a sister and a wonderful aunt at your farm."

"And another sister who lives in Portland—what's your brother like?"

"He's the charming one. Never married, at least so far. Women love him. Sometimes too much. Growing up, he was always in trouble. To this day, he's the one who tends to get himself in difficult situations."

"And you...?"

He fell back across the bed, tugging on her hand until she fell back beside him. Together, they stared up through the gnarled canopy of aspen branches, hands still entwined. "I was always on the straight and narrow. The summer I graduated college, I married the girl I'd been dating since our freshman year."

"Destination wedding, right? Someplace tropical—or wait. Scratch that. Some snooty private East Coast social club."

"You're good."

"Hey. I'm a writer. It's my job to read people, to figure out who they are and what makes them tick." She gave his hand a squeeze. "And where were we? Right. Everything was perfect. Top of your class at one of the best colleges in the country. You made your college sweetheart your bride, but somehow the marriage didn't work out..."

He made a low sound in the affirmative. "She missed her hometown and I'm in the family company. I like what I do. In less than five years, I'll be taking the leadership position. I just wasn't willing to give it up, to move away from *my* hometown, to find a new job where she wanted to be."

"Kids?"

"No."

Payton turned her head to study his profile. "But you were a true husband and you really tried."

He looked at her, his eyes shadowed, full of things he wouldn't say because they had rules and he played it on the straight and narrow. "Yeah. I tried. She tried. But the harder we tried, the clearer it became that there was something missing— something beyond the fact that she wanted to go home to her family and I wanted to stay where we were. We lacked that connection my parents have. They've been married for thirty years, and sometimes they still look at each other like the rest of the world doesn't even exist."

"I love that."

He chuckled. "You love that sometimes to this day I want to tell my mom and dad to get a room?"

"Oh, yeah. I love it a lot—the idea that two people can find each other and it's just somehow right, you know? Whatever happens, whatever life throws at them, they work it out. They're right for each other. Right for a lifetime. I envy you, to have grown up with parents who love each other deeply. I never had that. My mother married once. He's the father of my oldest sister, the one who lives in Portland."

"Once? You mean the marriage didn't last?"

"That is exactly what I mean. My mother cheated. She broke that poor man's heart. He ran off, abandoned everything, including his daughter, my sister. For my mother, it was always one man after another, but she never got married again. My second-born sister never really knew her dad, either. He died when she was still very small. But at least he cared, sent money when he could and made my mother put his last name on the birth certificate."

"And *your* dad?"

"Never met him, have no clue who he was. My mother told me different stories about him and why he wasn't in the picture. Mostly, she claimed that she didn't know who the lucky man was and didn't care. I didn't want to believe her. I waited and waited for him to finally come looking for me, but he never showed up."

"That's rough." Holding her gaze, he asked, "Your mother never gave you any information about him?"

"No. And she didn't give me much opportunity to ask her about him. She drifted in and out of our lives. Sometimes, she would stay at the family farm for weeks. Sometimes, she would disappear for months at a stretch. She died of hepatitis when I was ten."

Shifting onto his side to face her, Easton propped up on an elbow and rested his head on his hand. She mirrored him. They just looked at each other for a while. It was nice. Cozy.

Gently, he tucked a curl of hair behind her ear. "That must have been tough for you, first not getting to know your dad and then losing your mom so young."

"Yeah. I was bitter about not having a dad. And my mom was only in her thirties when she died. Luckily, my sisters and I always had our aunt Marilyn—Auntie M, as we call her. Auntie M never had kids herself and she was meant to be a mom. So we got lucky that way."

He leaned in. Their lips met. She could lie here forever, stretched across this big bed, kissing him.

"Tell me about the grown-up you," he said. "Serious relationships?"

"I've had boyfriends. A few. I'm my mother's daughter, though—I prefer to keep things light and fun with a guy. I like to think I'm more responsible than she was, at least. I know my limitations, I guess you could say. I never intend to have children and I never have unprotected sex. I like the single life. I have a lot I want to do and zero desire to get too distracted by a man."

"The ultimate independent woman, right?"

She chuckled. "You're the opposite of me, aren't you?"

"Not sure how to answer that—but yeah, my relationships with women have always been..." He seemed to be trying to choose the right word.

"Exclusive?"

"Yes. I had a girlfriend in middle school, and a high school sweetheart..."

She finished for him. "And then your wife, whom you met in college," she finished for him. "Did you save yourself for marriage?"

His mouth kicked up at one corner. "No."

"Ah. I'm guessing your first was the girlfriend in high school?"

"Yes." His eyes darkened. "Is it fair to ask about *your* first time?"

"Absolutely. I was sixteen. His name is Kyle. I've known Kyle practically since birth. We're still friends to this day."

"Already, I hate Kyle."

She laughed. "You shouldn't. He's a sweetheart. He has a small farm not far from our family farm and his passion is beekeeping."

Easton made a low, growly sound. "I don't want to hear another word about Kyle."

"Territorial, hmm?"

"That's right. You better watch out. It would be far too easy for me to become serious about you."

"No worries. I'm not going to let that happen— and neither are you."

"Right," he said ruefully. "And in the time we do have together, we need to make the best of every moment." He wrapped those wonderful arms around her and rolled to his back, pulling her on top of him.

For the next hour, she forgot everything—the chapter she should have finished the afternoon before, how tired she would be at the crack of dawn when she dragged her sleep-deprived body out to feed the goats and the chickens. In Easton's arms, she let her real life go.

There was only this moment, this magic. Only Easton and the feel of his hands on her body, the taste of his mouth, the scent of him, soap and man and something faintly, temptingly spicy.

The time went by much too fast. At four, same as last night, she slipped out from under the warm cocoon of blankets and put on her clothes. Perched on the side of the bed to pull on her socks, she said, "Before I get out of here, we do need to talk about the rules."

His warm hand closed on her shoulder. He gave a tug and she let herself fall backward, so her head was in his lap. Oh, man, he was beautiful, wearing nothing, with bedhead, gazing down at her through narrowed eyes. "It's about the lounge, right?"

She nodded up at him, grinning a little as she felt him hardening next to her ear. "Don't try to change the subject."

"I'm not. Ignore that." His voice was flat.

"Um, ahem." She told her dirty mind to cut it out and focus on the rules. "Of course you should come in the lounge whenever you want to. You're a guest of the inn, after all."

"But…"

"Easton, we can't hang out together in there. Midge really could pop in at any time. I can't afford to—"

"—lose your crappy job. I remember."

That kind of pissed her off. Whatever his "business" was that had brought him to Heartwood, the guy had money. His clothes, his watch, his haircut, his job that he loved in the "family company." Everything about him spoke quietly, comfortably of money.

"Yeah, well, some people have to take crappy jobs to realize their goals in life." She sat up and put on her other sock, followed by her shoes.

As she stood, he tried to call her back. "Payton."

"I have to go." She made it three steps before his arms went around her.

"I'm sorry." He buried his nose in her neck.

She let herself lean back against him, into his heat and strength. "You realize you stopped me on the way to the door last night, too."

"Yeah. I don't want you to go. Your leaving brings out the jackass in me."

"Quell that sucker."

He took her by the shoulders and turned her to face him. "Look at me."

Reluctantly, she raised her gaze to meet his. "What?"

"I won't hang around in the lounge during your shift."

"Thank you." She tried to ease away.

He held on. "Tonight?"

"Yes." She kissed him. How could she not? The man was irresistible.

He lifted his head only to bend close again and run his nose up the side of her neck. Fluttery creatures took flight in her belly as his warm breath tickled her ear. "When do you get a day off?"

"Easton, I don't have a lot of spare time, you know?"

"You keep saying that."

"It's actually true."

"Could you please just answer my question?" He had her by the shoulders now and held her a little away so that he could pin her with a look.

She surrendered the information. "Okay. I'm off Sunday and Monday."

"Spend them with me. We'll go somewhere— Hood River, maybe, if you want to stick close to town. Or Portland. Or even one of those cute towns along the coast. Just you and me for two whole days. We can hike somewhere, hold hands and go window shopping, just be together and not have to keep an eye on the time."

She shouldn't. She had page goals to hit and there was never a shortage of work on the farm.

"Stop thinking," he commanded.

"Oh, so you like a brainless woman."

"And stop deflecting. We don't have forever.

We need to make the most of our week. Just say yes…"

"You're impossible."

"Just say yes."

She wrinkled her nose at him. "Why can't I say no to you?"

"That's a yes—am I right?"

"Yeah. It's a yes." He kissed her again and then finally let her go.

The next night, Friday, true to his word, he came to the lounge for dinner and then left. After her shift, they spent two glorious hours crawling all over each other.

Saturday night he ate somewhere else, but he was waiting when she climbed the stairs to his suite. She fell into his arms. They made love three times and then talked for a while.

She liked talking to him almost as much as she enjoyed rolling around naked with him. He just might be the perfect man and she found it harder and harder to think of saying goodbye to him when the time came.

After morning chores on Sunday, Payton joined her sister and her aunt at Marilyn's house. Sunday breakfast had become something of a family tradition for the three of them in the past year, ever since Payton dropped out of Portland State and came back home to live.

They sat in the cozy kitchen where she'd eaten almost all her breakfasts growing up. Payton devoured her aunt's famous French toast casserole with marionberry syrup. Auntie M made the best coffee, French drip, rich and dark. Payton liked it with a fat dollop of whipped cream floating on top.

After they'd eaten their fill, Payton took their plates to the sink and poured them all a second cup.

When she sat down again, Josie shoved a hank of long, wildly curling strawberry blonde hair back off her face and said, "Okay. What's up? You look beat." Under the table, as if to punctuate her words, Josie's rescue Dutch Shepherd mix, Tinkerbell, yawned loudly.

Payton reached down and scratched Tink's short brindle coat. With a soft whine, the dog gave her fingers a lick. "So, it's like this." She straightened in her chair and had a sip of coffee. "I met a guy…"

Josie hid a smile. "Ah."

Auntie M beamed outright. "Wonderful. You've been working nonstop. It's lovely you've met someone, sweetie."

"It's not serious." She felt almost guilty saying it—which was absurd. It *wasn't* serious. It *couldn't* be serious. Both she and Easton understood that. "And he's only in town till Thursday."

Josie sipped coffee and then raised her mug to Payton. "Savor every moment."

Payton pretended to fan herself as she muttered, "You have no idea…"

Josie sighed. "Too true. Some of us have all the luck—what's his name?"

"Easton."

"Easton who?" Auntie M's green eyes twinkled.

"Just Easton—and the thing is, I was kind of hoping you two would be okay if I ran away with him for today and tomorrow, while I'm off from the lounge."

Her aunt and her sister shared a grin. "Go," they said in unison.

But then Auntie M frowned. "You sure this Easton person is safe?"

"I am." She said it with no hesitation. She didn't know his last name, but she trusted him implicitly. Go figure.

Auntie M read her mind. "Even though he has no last name?"

"She's right." Josie, ever the mother hen, just had to put her two cents in. "We at least hope you'll tell us where you're going and give us a call when you get there."

Payton was ready for that. Last night and Friday night, between toe-curling bouts of lovemaking, she and Easton had made their plans. "We're not going far, staying in Hood River, at that little B and B on Eugene Street."

"Sounds wonderful." Auntie M was all smiles.

Josie nodded. "Just call me when you get there."

When Payton arrived at the Cherry Tree Inn, Easton was waiting for her, leaning against that black sports car, arms crossed over his chest. His grin got wider as she climbed out of her trusty old Toyota Tacoma.

She ran to him. He picked her up and twirled her around. Her head spun as her feet touched the ground again—and then spun some more when he took her lips in a lingering kiss.

"Grab your bag," he said when he lifted his mouth from hers. "Let's get settled in."

Settling in entailed a long, satisfying encounter in their suite's big, comfy bed.

"Hungry?" he asked sometime after noon.

First, she called Josie and gave her their room number as she'd promised she would. Then they went out for lunch at a bar and grill on the river. Later, they shopped. She bought a handmade necklace for Auntie M and some hammered-copper earrings for Josie. At the Waucoma Bookstore, she found a biography of Justice Ruth Bader Ginsburg for her oldest sister, Alexandra. Alex worked long hours trying to make partner at the law offices of Kauffman, Judd and Tisdale.

It was a gorgeous day, clear and surprisingly warm. They went back to the B and B to drop off their purchases and have a glass of wine out on the patio, which had a perfect view of Mount Hood cloaked in its year-round mantle of snow.

"The mountain is out," she said and touched her glass of wine to his. It was a local expression. On a clear day like today, you could see Mount Hood from a hundred miles away.

That night they made love for hours. The next day, she slept until nine in the morning—gloriously late for a farm girl. They grabbed a quick breakfast, made the half-hour drive to the Hamilton Mountain Trailhead on the Washington side of the Columbia River and hiked for a while. He took several pictures of her posing with snowcapped Mount Adams in the background and one of the two of them on the sturdy footbridge that crossed Hardy Falls.

For dinner that evening, they chose a great little Italian restaurant right on the Columbia River. Later, in bed, they streamed *Suicide Squad* and cuddled like two people who'd been together forever.

She rested her head on his shoulder and thought how, in three days, he would be gone, back to the job he loved in the family company somewhere far away. Or maybe not so far. She would never know. She snuggled in closer to him, kind of missing him already.

And how pointless was that? To get all sad and gloomy when he was right here in bed with her.

On the flat-screen over the fireplace, Margot Robbie wielded Harley Quinn's baseball bat as the Suicide Squad kicked a lot of ass and blew up most of Midway City. The gunshots and explosions became nothing more than background noise as she lectured herself about her goals, her plans, all the ways she wasn't going to let any man—not even *this* man—lead her astray.

And besides, he felt the same way she did. Timing did matter and right now, for both of them, the timing sucked for getting romantically entangled.

He muted the flat-screen. "Okay, what?"

"Huh?"

"You're not watching the movie. You're about a thousand miles away. What's wrong?"

She bit the corner of her lip and considered whether or not to just go ahead and tell him that she liked him way too much, that she didn't want to say goodbye on Thursday, after all.

But then, well…

*Uh-uh. No way.* She refused to go there. It was only a fantasy that they would find true love together and make a life side by side.

She pulled him nice and close. Sliding her hand down between them, she wrapped her fingers around his hardening length. "I was just thinking that I'm not really in the mood for *Suicide Squad*, after all."

He pointed the remote again and the screen went black. "What then?" He was grinning.

"Let me show you exactly what I have in mind…"

After that, she kept her thoughts in check and her eyes on the prize of her own independence, on the books she would write and the life she had planned.

This thing with Easton was only an interlude, a single week with a wonderful man, a hot, rejuvenating break from constantly pushing herself to do her part at the farm, stay awake in the lounge and make every page of her trilogy soar.

Tuesday morning, he kissed her goodbye while she was still in bed. "Relax," he said. "I've already settled up at the front desk. Give me at least a half-hour head start. Because if you go first, or if we leave at the same time, I'm going to be tempted to follow you and find out where you live."

She grabbed him close and kissed him again, glad in spite of herself that he found a forbidden future with her as seductive as she found the impossible dream of one with him.

At home on the farm, Tink ran out to greet her and Auntie M emerged from her cottage, crossed the stretch of lawn and gave her a welcoming hug. "Did you have a good time?"

"The best."

"Not that I really needed to ask." Wearing a smirk, her aunt adjusted the headband that held back her chin-length silver hair. "You've got stars in your eyes and color in your cheeks. Young love. Oh, my, yes…"

Payton only smiled. "I had a really good time."

That night and the night after flew by much too fast. At 4:00 a.m. Thursday morning, it was time for her and Easton to say goodbye.

Payton rose from the big bed and put on her clothes. Easton said nothing. Sitting up against the pillows, the sheet pulled to his waist, he watched her.

She tried to keep a smile on her face as she put on her underwear and zipped up her jeans, sat on the edge of the bed to don her socks and her shoes.

Finally, she stood and turned to face him. "Well. I, um…" She really had no idea what to say next.

He tossed back the covers and swung his feet to the rug. Taking her by the shoulders, he pulled her close.

His mouth came down on hers. They must have shared a thousand kisses in the week just past— more than a thousand. Ten thousand. But it didn't matter how many kisses he gave her; she wanted another one. And another one after that.

He caught her bottom lip between his teeth and bit down hard enough she tasted blood—not that she cared. He could bite her lip clean through.

She would still only want to kiss him again.

"Let's stop this silliness," he said darkly. "Give me your phone."

She blinked up at him, bewildered. Bizarrely confused. "Why?"

"Why do you think?"

"Easton. Come on. Please don't do—"

"I want to see you again. I don't want this to be the end of it."

"But it is the end of it. We have an agreement and I mean to stick by it."

"Payton, come on. We can't just walk away."

"That was the point."

"I don't care. I'm not spending the rest of my life wondering where you are."

"You'll get over it."

"Stop it. That's just mean."

"It's what we agreed. The last thing either of us needs is to get involved with someone new right now."

"New? This doesn't feel new. Not anymore. It feels…real, Payton. It feels like something we shouldn't just let go."

"Easton. It's been a week, a great week. That's

what I signed on for and that's all I'm ready for.
If you look in your heart and be honest, I think
you'll see that you're in the same situation as me."

"I don't care." His face was a portrait of unhappy rebellion. "This thing with us, it's right.
We'll regret it if we just walk away."

"But it's not right. You said it yourself. Your
divorce has been final for what—a week and a
half now? I'm twenty-three years old and for the
first time in my life I know where I'm going and
what I want. I refuse to get distracted from my
goal now that I finally have one."

His mouth twisted. "So I'm a distraction?"

She put her hand against his heart and spoke
softly, urgently. "Timing does matter, Easton.
And the timing now, with us…?"

He winced and loosened his painful grip on
her shoulders. "I'll give you that. I know the timing's not ideal."

"We need to let go. It's what we agreed on from
the first and it's the best way. I know that it is. I
think you do, too."

He released her. They faced each other without touching. "All right." He said it flatly. It was
exactly what she'd asked him for. So why did his
capitulation make her heart hurt so bad?

Their gazes held. She forced a smile—and it
helped. His answering smile lit her up from the

inside. "You are amazing and this was the best week ever."

He granted her a slow nod. "God, I will miss you."

She made herself turn, grab her jacket and put it on. Settling the strap of her bag on her shoulder, she couldn't just leave it at a pure and simple goodbye. "And, um, well, who knows what the future will bring, right? You might end up back in Heartwood someday. We might reconnect."

He laughed then. It wasn't a happy sound. "And how will I find you?"

"It's a small town."

"Payton, I…"

She stopped him with a slow shake of her head. "No. Please don't. We need to let it be now. It was perfect and I loved every minute of it."

"Damn it, Payton. I loved it, too, and I—"

"No more. Let's just leave it." She backed toward the door. "Let me go," she pleaded in barely a whisper.

"All right." The two little words came out bleak, gravelly.

She turned, flipped back the security bar and pulled open the door, whirling to face him one last time—because she just couldn't bear to leave without adding like a hopeless fool, "And hey, you never know. There is such a thing as fate, after all. If it's meant to be, we'll find each other and—"

"Just go," he said flatly.

He was right. She'd already beat him over the head with the rules. What more was there to say?

Backing out onto the landing, she pulled the door shut on his grim, closed-off face. For an endless count of ten, she stood there, frozen in place, longing to knock on the door, praying he might fling it open so that she could throw herself into his arms and admit she couldn't do it, couldn't just walk away the way they'd agreed.

She needed his phone number, after all. She needed his address and his promise that this wasn't the end of it, that they would see each other again, that he would come back to her, that she would go to him wherever it was that he made his home.

But she didn't knock. The door remained shut.

Zipping up her jacket, she resettled her purse on her shoulder and turned for the stairs.

## Chapter Four

*Six months later...*

In her bedroom at Wild Rose Farm, Payton glanced up from the leather-bound blank book she'd ordered on Etsy two weeks before.

She sat at the small table she'd pulled up to the window so that she could look out at the tangle of Nootka and Woods' roses that grew in front of the porch on either side of the front steps. Both varieties were in bloom, the petals delicate wheels in two shades of pink, their sweet, faint scent tempting her through the open window.

Across the way, she could see her aunt's cottage, the pale blue wood siding in need of a fresh coat of paint. Tink snoozed on the mat in front of her aunt's turquoise front door. Farther out, the cherry, pear and apple orchards bloomed in a riot of pink and white. Lording over all of it, off in the distance, Mount Hood, covered in its cloak of snow, loomed in splendor.

A tiny foot poked at her from the inside. "Ow." She rubbed her swollen belly. "Easy there, mister." Spreading both hands on either side of the fat, hard ball that used to be her flat stomach, she spoke fondly to the little ones within her. "Neither of you is getting out for a few months yet. Settle down, please. I love that you're active, but you don't need to spend all your time kicking your mama."

Her gaze strayed upward to the blank book spread open on the table in front of her. She may have finished the chores Josie and Auntie M would allow her to tackle around the farm since she'd started waddling like a duck, but she still had at least two chapters of *Lord of Ice and Shadow* to write today.

And before that, she needed to make a start at filling this blank book.

She picked up her pen and brought the tip to the empty page, where she scrawled the day and date and then the salutation: *"Dear Easton..."*

Sadness welled within her. She almost tossed the pen down and buried her head in her hands.

But no. Pregnant-lady hormones were not taking over now. She'd bought this journal when all the constructive options failed her. It was too little too late and she damn well knew it.

But hey. Some said confession was good for the soul.

I've been sitting here staring out the window for way too long and it's not helping. I don't even know where to start. So I guess I'll just jump right in and fill this blank book with my guilt and apologies.

Yes, I do realize that I have only myself to blame for the fact that I have no idea how to reach you. Leave it to me to repeatedly refuse to bend the rules of our time together—me, who until you, broke the rules every chance she got. Leave it to me to suddenly get a backbone at exactly the wrong moment. And leave it to me to count on fate to bring us back together at some distant, perfect time.

How could I not have known better? I am a writer, after all. Every writer worth her salt knows that fate's a mean bitch with rotten tricks up both sleeves.

So here's the thing. I'm pregnant—six months along. And I am big. I'm still carrying high, as they say, but to the inexperienced eye, I look like I'm about to go into labor any minute now. That's because I'm having twin boys. Yes, they are yours. And I HAVE tried to find you. Too bad I don't have a clue where to start.

Oh, Easton, I kind of hate myself. I have no desire to keep your children from you—I swear to you, I don't. And if you're reading this, well, that means I finally did find you, and I do need you to know that I never meant to do to you or to our sons what my mom did to me and my dad—whoever he was. You need to know that I will tell the boys that you are a great guy and I messed up when you left, that I refused to take your digits when you offered them and then I couldn't find you. I'll make it crystal clear to them that I had an agreement with you and I wouldn't budge from it, though you repeatedly asked me to ease up on my rules.

I know I keep saying I'm sorry. I know it doesn't help, my being sorry over something as important as this. Sorry doesn't make it right when you will have children you may never get to meet.

After the home test came out positive, I went to my doctor and had the test confirmed. By then, I knew I had to go to Midge, that she was the best and pretty much only hope I had of finding you. It took me a while to make myself deal with her.

But finally, in January, I did deal with her. I was three months along then and still had the job at the lounge. I went to her and laid it all out for her, told her that you and I had spent a week together, that I was pregnant with your babies. I begged her to let me see the record of your visit.

Remember how I said Midge hates me? I

wasn't wrong. She lectured me about birth control. Completely pissed me off—as if I would ever have unprotected sex. But I didn't argue with her. I mean, what good would it do, anyway, for me to get down in the weeds about how we used a condom every time and one of them must have failed?

I stood there and took it as she shook a finger at me and said how it was time for me to "lie in the bed I had made for myself." Like she was the hateful, completely unchristian Mother Superior in a bad B movie that takes place in some gloomy convent circa 1953.

Then she said that it was against the law for her to give out a guest's personal information to anyone—and she wouldn't give it to me, anyway, even if she could.

About then, I started talking back. It wasn't pretty. I told Midge exactly what she could do with her self-righteous attitude and mean-spirited moral superiority.

She fired me. Big surprise.

All that to say, yeah. Dead end on the Midge front. I tried social media—if you're on Twitter or Insta or LinkedIn or Facebook, I couldn't find you—no surprise, I know. How would I find you when I don't know your last name, what you do or where you live?

I even hired a private investigator, but he warned me that without a picture, a last name or a possible location, he probably wouldn't get far. He was right. Up till now, anyway, he hasn't come up with any information that might help me find you. I can't believe I didn't at least get one picture of you. Or ask you to send me the ones you took of us that day we went hiking—but how could you send me those pictures when I stubbornly refused to give you my number or even an email address?

Anyway, Easton, I was wrong. I know it. So wrong, not to arrange a way to find you when I had the chance. At the time, I felt bleak and determined and strong. I just knew that I was doing the right thing to walk away as we'd agreed.

Now, though? Now, what I did merely seems terminally imprudent, thoughtless, irresponsible and unwise. All qualities I've been well known for—but never so much as when I think back on the moment that we said goodbye, when I remember the last chance you tried so hard to give me.

The last chance to which I said no. I said no and I walked out the door.

And that is why I bought this empty journal, to fill it with true stories of your two sons. I promise to write in it frequently, so that when we do meet again—yes, I'm determined to be positive about this—I will at least be able to hand you a record of your children's lives so far.

It's not enough and I know it. But maybe it will help you to know them, maybe it will prepare you, at least marginally, for the fatherhood you neither expected nor asked for. I knew you for a week, and I admired you so. Maybe I shouldn't be so certain that you will want your sons and love them and help them to grow up to be good men. Just like you.

But I am certain, Easton. And I hope that the day I finally give you this journal, there won't be much in it—because that would mean that somehow, before the boys were even born, I found a way to get in contact with you, after all.

*Four and a half years later...*

Easton had just started unpacking when Weston called. "Just checking to make sure you got in all right," his twin said.

Easton stuck in his Bluetooth earbuds, slid the phone into a pocket and scooped up a stack of T-shirts from one of the suitcases sitting open on the bed. There were five suitcases. He would be living between Heartwood and Seattle for the next several months. This project was his first major acquisition as CEO of Wright Hospitality, and he intended to keep a close eye on its progress. "I'm settling in, unpacking as we speak."

"Trip okay?" Weston asked.

"Uneventful." He'd driven down in his favorite car, a BMW Alpina XB7.

"How's the rental house?"

Easton carried the stack of T-shirts to the big bureau next to the window and stuck it in a drawer. "It's a five-minute drive from here to the property, way more space than I need. Indoor-outdoor fireplace, river views."

"So no complaints?"

"It's fine. I'll be meeting with the design and construction teams first thing tomorrow."

"Big dreams finally coming true," said his brother, meaning Easton's long-delayed plans for acquiring, expanding, renovating and rebranding the Heartwood Inn as a Wright Hospitality property. Their father and the board had passed on the project five years ago when Easton first proposed it. But with Easton at the helm now and Weston backing him up as CFO, the board had agreed to take another look. This time the vote had gone in Easton's favor.

Easton continued hanging clothes in the closet and filling the bureau drawers as he and his brother went over the main points for Friday's on-site meetings.

"So everything's under control," said Weston as they were winding down the conversation.

"As much as it ever is."

"You never know. Maybe in your copious free time, you'll get to reconnect with an old flame." Weston was razzing him. Four years ago, on a long night out over one too many whiskey sours, Easton had told his twin about Payton—about the week they'd spent together that Easton couldn't seem to forget, about how good it was with her. He explained the rules they'd agreed on and how she'd made him stick by them, how he'd come back to Heartwood six months later hoping to find her again, only to learn that she'd married some other guy and moved away.

Easton answered his brother in a bored tone, "I have no idea what you're talking about."

"Liar, liar."

Easton grinned to himself. "I thought I told you she got married and doesn't live in Heartwood anymore."

"Hey, it's been years. People get divorced. Sometimes, they get divorced and move back to the old hometown."

Easton got his brother's message loud and clear. Miranda, Easton's ex-wife, had gone back home to New York. Two years ago, she'd remarried. Recently, he'd heard from a mutual friend that she was living her best life on the Upper East Side, pregnant with her first child. "Don't be smug, little brother." Weston had been born eleven minutes after Easton, thus making Easton the elder of the two. Easton enjoyed rubbing that in now and then.

"I'm not. I keep myself open to all the possibilities—as should you. You'll be hanging around in Heartwood a lot in the next few months. Anything could happen."

"Ever the optimist."

Weston chuckled. "That's right. Good things all the time."

After they said goodbye, Easton finished unpacking. He got a beer from the fridge, which had been fully stocked in anticipation of his arrival, and went out to sit on the deck with the fire going as the sun went down.

*Payton…*

Was it weird that he'd never gotten over her? Probably.

After all this time, he still thought of her, still recalled the feel of her in his arms, the taste of her pretty mouth, how she made him laugh and made him think. Sometimes, like tonight, he couldn't stop himself from imagining what might have been five years ago if only he'd somehow convinced her to give up her damn rules.

\* \* \*

"Mom." A small, grubby hand tugged on the hem of her big white sweater as Payton handed a customer a bag containing two fat stalks of celery and three bunches of carrots with the tops still on. Every Saturday, from the middle of May to the end of October, Payton sold Wild Rose Farm produce at the Heartwood Saturday Market.

She shot her son a chiding glance and gave the customer a big smile as she took a business card from the holder by the cashbox. "This is the last Saturday market of the season, but check out our website. You can place orders there and you can order by phone, too."

The customer took the card. "Perfect. Thanks."

"Mom…" Penn gave another yank on her sweater as the customer moved on.

"What, Penn?"

"Boo!" Bailey, twelve minutes younger and every bit as full of energy and mischief as his brother, leaped out from under one of the other farm tables. Payton had three tables in the booth. She'd set them up in an upside-down U configuration and covered each one with crates of Wild Rose Farm produce.

Payton put up both hands. "Whoa. Scary!" She lowered her voice and reminded them softly, "And, boys, come on. Mama's workin' here. Stay in the booth and also out of the way."

"Can we go with Kyle?" Penn gazed up at her with a sweet, dewy-eyed smile.

"Puleeease," coaxed Bailey. "Kyle said it was okay."

The booth where Kyle Huckston offered honey in jars, squeeze bottles and on the comb was four booths down from hers. She wouldn't be able to see the twins if she let them go over there. The boys had a lot of energy, vivid imaginations and occasional boundary issues. Letting them out of her sight at the Saturday market could too easily result in disaster. Plus, her lifelong friend—and briefly, more than a year and a half ago now, her fiancé— was here to sell honey, not babysit her children.

"Kyle's working," she said, careful to make eye contact with each of the boys in turn. She'd learned the hard way that if she only looked at one of them when she gave instructions, the other just might feel free to commit whatever mayhem popped into his head. "I want you two to stay here, please."

"But Kyle said it was okay!" insisted Bailey, giving her the big eyes. He and his brother loved hanging with Kyle.

"Wait. When did Kyle say that?"

"Just now," replied Penn. "He's right there."

Sure enough, Kyle stood a few feet away and she hadn't even noticed him, let alone seen the boys talking to him. Really, there needed to be two of her on market days—one to keep the boys in line and one to run the Wild Rose booth. "Hey, Kyle…"

"Hey, gorgeous. I've got Dad with me today and you know how he is." Payton did know. Tom Huckston loved to sell honey. And talk. "Come on," Kyle coaxed. "Last market of the season and I've got nothing to do. I'm happy to take them to my booth for a while."

The boys started jumping up and down, making prayer hands. "Please, Mom…"

"*Can* we, Mom?"

"Kyle *says* it's okay, Mom…"

"Settle," she commanded firmly. They were way too cute. She wanted to grab them and hug them, but they were also a lot like Tink. They responded best to firm, clear commands.

The boys stopped jumping and stared up at her hopefully through two sets of vivid blue eyes— eyes they'd inherited from the father she sometimes feared they would never get to meet.

Penn solemnly nodded. "We are settled. May we *please* go with Kyle?"

"Yes—say thank you to Kyle."

"Thank you, Kyle!" they cried in unison.

She turned to her friend. "I owe you."

He shrugged. "What are friends for? Plus, us guys have to stick together." He signaled the twins with a wave. "Come on, you two. Let's go see what Grandpa Tom is up to." Everyone in town called Kyle's dad Grandpa Tom.

She thanked Kyle again and he left with the boys, who bounced around him like a couple of jumping beans, both of them talking at the same time.

She felt a little wistful as she watched the three of them go. Her boys were only four, and yet she could feel their need for a father figure. That need had her halfheartedly wishing her ill-fated engagement to Kyle had worked out. She loved Kyle and always would. He was such a great guy, trustworthy, handsome, kind…

But the two of them as a couple?

Never meant to be.

And now Kyle had Olga. He was in love and happy with his girlfriend of almost a year now.

The next half hour passed quickly. Payton sold produce, chatted with her customers and wondered in the back of her mind how many Saturdays she'd stood right here under the white canopy in the Wild Rose Farm booth, thinking about Easton, silently lecturing herself to let it go, get over it. Reminding herself how she needed to accept that she would never see him again, how she needed to face the bleak fact that, just like their mother before them, her children would never know their father.

Dear God, that depressed her. Could fate really be so cruel?

She hated going down that dark road in her head, hated it enough that, just to lift her spirits a little, she would inevitably start fantasizing how someday she would glance up and see him walking toward her.

"Thank you, Payton." Delia Morton, who owned and ran Heartwood Home Cookin' on Center Street, accepted the bags of sweet peppers, winter squash and carrots Payton had just filled for her. Delia regularly called the farm to place large orders for her restaurant, but she often dropped by the market on Saturdays. When she did, she always dropped in at the Wild Rose booth. "How's your aunt Marilyn?"

"Unstoppable as ever."

"Good, good. How's the book going?" Delia asked the question with a big, proud smile. Like most folks in town, the café owner loved that a local girl had "made good" with her little writing hobby.

"I've just started a new book, so I'm kind of feeling my way through it right now."

"What's the name of this one?"

"Titles can change, but as of now it's *Queen of Jade and Sorrow*."

Delia frowned. "It sounds sad." Payton's publisher thought so, too, and that meant the title most likely would change. "Is it sad?" Delia asked.

"Some parts, yeah."

"But exciting, right? Sword fights and knife throwing and those sexy archers with the horns and the hooves instead of feet?"

"You'd better believe it."

"And there's romance—am I right?"

"Always, Delia. I promise you."

"That's what I want to hear—and how's Josie?" Delia wore a prim little smile now. Like Payton and their mother before them, Josie was pregnant with no man in sight. Josie's pregnancy, however, was in no way accidental. She'd chosen to have intrauterine insemination.

Payton answered the café owner with a superlative. "Josie's amazing, as always." Because her sister was the best of the best. "We all three pitch in at the farm, but Josie's the brains, the work ethic and the organization behind it all."

"She's not working *too* hard, I hope?"

Josie LeClaire always worked too hard. A doctor of veterinary medicine, she ran the farm and also worked part-time for Heartwood Animal Clinic. "I promise you, Delia, Josie's feeling good and doing well."

"I'm so glad to hear that. You tell her for me that…" As Delia spoke, the woman behind her with a cabbage in one hand and a head of broccoli in the other, let out an audible sigh. "Oops!" Though well into her sixties, Delia giggled like a preteen. "I'm sorry, hon. I do get carried away— you take care now, Payton."

Payton thanked the café owner again and Delia moved along. The sighing woman paid and left, as did the couple behind her. By then, it was after two and the market closed at three. Payton began combining boxes of produce, stacking the empties under the farm tables, getting things organized, ready to go. When Kyle returned, he would help her fold up the long tables and get them loaded up.

She didn't know what, exactly, alerted her, but she had the oddest feeling that someone was watching her. One second, she was lifting a freshly emptied crate off a table and the next, she set the crate back down, braced her hands on the table and scanned the shoppers strolling by her booth.

*Easton.*

She blinked several times in rapid succession as her heart raced and sweat broke out on her upper lip and under her arms. Surely, she must be seeing things.

A silly whimper of sound escaped her as she narrowed her eyes, squinting at the man she'd actually thought might be him.

The man did not change.

In black jeans, a dark crew-neck shirt and a tan leather jacket, he stood between her booth and the jewelry booth across the way. Those eyes—her sons' eyes—were locked right on her.

No. It couldn't be. It just wasn't possible.

She scrunched her own eyes completely shut and willed the illusion to fade away.

But when she looked again, he hadn't faded in the least.

On the contrary, he looked painfully real. He also started walking straight for her.

Her stomach heaved and her head spun. For a moment, she felt certain she would throw up, or pass out from the way her head had started spinning. But she sucked in a couple of slow, deep breaths and her stomach settled, though marginally. The dizziness seemed less, too.

"You okay?" He stood right in front of her, with only a farm table between them. Concern drew his dark gold eyebrows together.

"I… Fine. Yes!" God. She sounded almost as freaked as she felt. "Just, um, you know. Surprised to see you." He looked so good—lean and broad shouldered, the way she remembered. A little older, with faint crow's-feet beside his eyes now.

He held her gaze, steady. Sure. "Long time, huh?"

She gulped. "Yeah." This did not in any way feel real. She had to resist the urge to reach across the table, give his big shoulder a quick squeeze, reassure herself that she hadn't somehow slipped off into an alternate reality where the long-lost father of her sons appeared out of nowhere at the Heartwood Saturday Market. "I—I can't believe you're actually h-here…" Now she was stuttering.

And the boys! What about the boys? Kyle could come wandering back with them any minute. She needed to keep that from happening until she'd had a chance to speak with Easton in private, to prepare him for the shocking news that he had four-year-old twin boys.

*Dear God in heaven…*

How could this be? Yes, it was her most cherished fantasy, to someday see him again. But in her fantasy, it was only the two of them, lost in each other's eyes…

Sheesh. *Get a grip, Payton.*

She lifted a hand to rake her hair back off her forehead, a purely nervous gesture, as she tried to figure out how to get a phone number from him and then make him leave.

He grabbed her wrist, and then caught her fingers.

She flinched. "What?"

"Sorry." He let go. "You're not wearing a ring."

"Easton. What are you talking about?"

"I'm surprised to see you here."

"What do you mean? I live here."

"And you're not married?"

"Uh, no."

"So then, it didn't work out?"

She stared at him, flummoxed. "It? What?"

"I'm making a hash of this. And you're right. It's none of my business."

"Wait." By then, she'd started to put it together. "You think I was married?" At his nod, she shook her head. "No. Uh-uh. I've never been married. Who told you that?"

Now he was the stunned one. Instead of answering her question, he asked another of his own. "And you never moved away?"

"No. Who said I was married? What made you think I'd moved away?"

"Ahem. 'Scuse me."

They both turned to look at the balding, pot-bellied man who just might have been standing there long enough to hear every word of their bizarre exchange.

Payton forced a smile. "Hi. May I help you?"

The guy wanted a crate of Josie's lovingly tended Cherokee Purple heirloom tomatoes and another of Yukon Gold potatoes. He had a credit card, so it only took a second to swipe it through her card reader. Both crates were cardboard. She let the guy have them. He stacked the tomatoes on top of the potatoes and off he went.

Way too aware of the seconds ticking by, praying that her sons wouldn't come bouncing back from the Huckston Honey booth before Easton moved on, she turned to him again. "So…"

"You're more beautiful than I remembered." He said it low, almost reverently, in exactly the tone she'd imagined him using in her fantasy of this meeting.

But this was no fantasy and she needed him gone—*after* she set up a private meeting with him. And got his phone number as she should have done five years ago.

Dear, sweet God in heaven, could this really be happening?

"I couldn't stop thinking of you," he said. "Six months after that week we had together, I came back to try to find you."

Her pulse lurched to a stop and she had trouble drawing air. How could he do this? How could he so perfectly enact her longtime fantasy of his sudden appearance here at the Saturday market? It seemed impossible. And he kept looking at her so hopefully. A single word escaped her. "No…" It came out in barely a whisper.

He moved back a step. "What? You're upset that I came looking for you?"

"No!" This time, the word erupted from her mouth, frantic and loud. She winced at the sound and tried to speak quietly. "Of course not. I just meant, well, I had no idea…" *Because I gave you no way to find me.* Guilt twisted in her belly like a rusty knife.

He was nodding. "Yeah, well, I came back hoping I might find you behind the bar at the Larch Tree Lounge."

"Six months after you left town would've been too late. I stopped working there three months before that." Because Midge had fired her for sleeping with a guest—him. Or maybe for being pregnant. Who could say exactly what went on in the mind of Midge Shanahan?

Easton said, "I asked the guy behind the bar about you. He said he was new in town and didn't know you or why you'd left the lounge. After that, I went to the manager."

And how much had Midge told him?

As if she'd asked the question out loud, he answered, "The Shanahan woman said you'd gotten married and moved away."

Payton managed a slow, careful breath. "Leave it to Midge."

"So then, the manager lied to me?"

"Yeah."

He stared at her as though hypnotized. Oh, she knew the feeling. It was nothing short of otherworldly, to see him again.

And what were they talking about?

Right. Midge. "Midge, um, died. Of acute appendicitis. Apparently, she refused to see a doctor. When she finally called an ambulance, it was too late. That was two years ago—which is sad, right? I mean, it's sad when people die…"

They stared at each other for several increasingly weird seconds—and then they both burst into totally inappropriate laughter, which they curtailed simultaneously.

"Sorry," she said.

"Me, too," he agreed.

They both put on somber expressions and she couldn't stop herself from adding, "The way I heard it, she was mean right up to the end. Not a happy woman, ever, apparently."

"Yeah," he said. "I get that about her."

For a good, long count of ten, they simply stared at each other.

Then he whispered, "I can't stop staring at you." Those eyes seemed to reach down inside her, stirring up the sweetest memories, making her burn for him. "I can't believe I've found you again—how about dinner, you and me, tonight?"

*He wants to see me again!* Her insides lit up with a million happy twinkle lights as her heart did something impossibly athletic inside her chest.

*Stop*, she sternly reminded herself. *Get a grip, Paytaytochip*, as her both of sisters used to say when they were kids. *This is not your starry-eyed romantic fantasy come true.*

She was the mother of his children—two sweet,

rambunctious boys who had lived four years of their lives without knowing him, thanks to her. She needed to tell him that he was a dad and she needed *not* to do it here. "Yes. Okay. Dinner would be great—someplace quiet, where we can talk."

He didn't miss a beat. "I'll pick you up." He gestured with both hands at the tent, the folding tables and what was left of the produce on them. "I take it you're still at the family farm?"

"I am, yeah."

He took one of the business cards. "Wild Rose Farm."

"That's us."

"It's amazing when you think about it, how careful we really were. If you'd mentioned the name of your farm just once, I could've found you so easily."

"Yeah." She felt…lost suddenly, dragged down by the weight of choices she'd made without the slightest consideration of the possible consequences. "But listen. I'll meet you." She named a small Italian place in town that had cozy private booths where she could say what he needed to hear without an audience.

He frowned and offered again, "I don't mind picking you up."

That couldn't happen. She had to be realistic; this could go any number of ways and she needed her own wheels in case it ended badly. "No, really. I'll meet you there."

They shared a long, intense look. And then he surrendered. "All right."

"I'll call and get us a booth." It was Saturday night, but a booth should be doable. "Seven?" she asked.

"I'll be there."

"Okay. See you then." She gave him a too-wide smile, hoping he would just take the hint and move on.

He did no such thing. Instead, he pulled out his phone, unlocked it and held it out to her. "Will you please give me your number?"

Feeling extra-awful for not having offered it to him before he had to ask for it, she accepted the phone and texted herself. Two words: Payton's phone. Her phone pinged in her pocket and she handed his phone back.

When he looked at her text, he asked ruefully, "Still no last name, huh?"

Her throat clutched. She wanted to babble excuses, to promise him she wasn't planning to stand him up or anything like that. But what good would excuses do?

And if he didn't leave soon, Kyle was bound to show up with the boys.

"It's Dahl," she said, took out her phone and texted him back, repeating the words as she typed them. "Payton Dahl. The restaurant is Barone's. It's right here in Heartwood." She texted that to him.

Barone's on Pine Street.

His phone pinged and he gave her a smile. "See you at seven."

She nodded. "I'll make the reservation in my name."

"It's so good to see you again." He said it quietly. Kind of intimately.

She liked that way too much. "Yes. Good to see you, too…"

He held up his phone and the business card, one in either hand. "And at least this time, no matter what happens, I'll know how to get in touch with you. See you at seven, Payton Dahl…"

And at last, he turned and walked away.

She watched him go. Feeling weak in the knees, her stomach in knots, she had no idea how he was going to react to the life-changing news she would have to deliver tonight.

## *Chapter Five*

In a daze, Easton headed for his car. He had her number. He knew her last name. He would see her tonight…

Five damn years. And after the Shanahan woman had lied right to his face, he'd believed her and pretty much given up hope of ever seeing Payton again.

But he'd never really forgotten her. No other woman compared. He'd known her for eight nights and those two glorious days in Hood River. A blink of an eye, really. And yet the memory of her stuck with him.

The reality, though, was so much better.

He stopped in midstride a few booths down from hers and tipped his head to the overcast sky. Who knew what would happen tonight? Maybe nothing. He shouldn't get his hopes up.

He wondered about the writing thing. Had that gone anywhere for her? He would ask her tonight. He had a lot of questions. He wanted to know everything about her.

It was all wide-open this time. The old rules didn't apply. She'd given him her digits and her last name. He could share whatever the hell he chose to share about himself. He could maybe visit her farm, find out if she ever sold that book she'd been writing.

Something rammed against his leg.

"Oops," said a child's voice. He looked down into a pair of bright blue eyes. "Sor-ry."

He steadied the kid with a hand on his small shoulder. "Be careful, there…"

"I will!" The kid turned, laughing. Easton watched him run to the nearest booth, which sold organic honey.

Another kid, who looked almost exactly like the first, appeared from around the side of the honey seller's tent.

Twins. They brought to mind his own childhood, him and Weston, bouncing balls of energy, laughing and roughhousing up and down their tree-lined street in Washington Park.

"Penn!" called the second boy.

"I'm here!"

"Stay close, boys," warned their father, a smiling, bearded lumberjack type in a plaid shirt and faded jeans who stood behind a broad table stacked with jars of honey. The bearded guy said something to the older man—the grandfather, no doubt—sitting beside him. The older man laughed as the twin boys ducked beneath the table.

*Kids*, thought Easton, and headed toward his car again. He'd always wanted a houseful of them. Sometimes lately he doubted he would ever have a single one.

But right now, he didn't feel doubtful about anything. The world seemed wide-open. Anything might happen.

Tonight, he would see Payton again. They had so much to catch up on. He couldn't wait.

He got to the restaurant fifteen minutes early. A homey little place with tables in the center and high-backed booths along both sides, Barone's Italian Restaurant smelled amazing. At the check-in podium, he gave Payton's name. A smiling dark-haired woman led him to a corner booth.

"Bread while you wait?" she asked.

He said yes to the bread and chose a nice bottle of wine.

Ten minutes later, he'd eaten half the bread and finished a glass of the wine. Nervous much? Chuckling to himself, he turned his wineglass by the stem and resisted the temptation to pour himself some more before Payton had even arrived.

The final minutes until seven crawled by with the speed of a drunken snail. But then he glanced over—and there she was at the door, all that wavy, bronze-streaked brown hair loose on her shoulders, wearing a short red sweater, skinny jeans and ankle boots, looking even better than she had in his fantasies the past five years.

He rose as she slid onto the bench across from him. "Hi."

"Hi." Her face was flushed. She dropped her bag next to her on the seat and set a book with a tooled leather cover down beside it.

"You brought something to read in case you get bored?" he teased.

She seemed breathless, suddenly. Those eyes, which could look gray or blue depending on her mood or maybe the light, shifted away and then back. "Of course not." And then she smiled again.

He forgot all about the book. "Wine?"

"Yes, please."

He poured for her and then allowed himself a second glass. She had a sip and hummed low in her throat. "It's really good."

The dark-haired woman returned. They ordered an antipasto and a couple of entrées.

When the woman left, Payton said, "I realized after you left today that you got my last name, but I forgot to get yours."

"It's Wright."

"With a *W*?"

"That's it."

"Easton Wright…" She blasted him with another dazzling smile. Was she nervous? Her face was flushed. "So tell me, Easton Wright, what brings you back to Heartwood?"

"Long story."

"I'm listening."

"I did mention four years ago that I work in my family's company, didn't I?"

"You did."

"We acquire, renovate and rebrand hotel properties. My father created the company Wright Hospitality thirty-six years ago. He's a big believer that anyone who runs a business should earn the job. Both my brother and I started at the bottom. We learned the hotel business from the ground up. Five years ago, I was still learning, kind of moving up the food chain with the understanding that I would eventually be running things, alongside my brother."

"Whose name is…?"

"Weston."

"Easton and Weston…"

"My mother chose our names. She thought it was cute. My dad tried to talk her out of it, but when Mom sets her heart on something, forget going in another direction. We're twins, Weston and me. I'm older by eleven minutes."

"Twins," she said, as though the news stunned her. "You're a twin…"

"That's right."

"Identical?"

"Yeah."

"It's random, not inherited," she said, as if that was somehow important. "To have identical twins, I mean."

"I'm aware of that," he replied, because, well, what else was there to say—and was something off with her? She seemed nervous.

Then again, he felt strangely anxious, too. It had been so long, yet the pull between them hadn't diminished at all. To him, the attraction felt stronger than ever and he found that kind of nerve-wracking.

She blinked. "Easton and Weston, huh? It *is* cute."

"As I have frequently reminded my mother, do not ever tell a man that his name is cute."

"Noted." She said it playfully, with a soft smile. And then she sucked in a slightly shaky breath.

He wanted to grab her hand, to offer comfort somehow—even though he had no idea why she might need comforting. "Is everything okay?"

"Yes!" She said it much too eagerly. "Fine, really—you were saying, about you and your brother and you coming back to Heartwood…?"

Okay, then, he thought. Message received. Whatever she had on her mind, she didn't want to talk about it—not now, anyway. "I'm CEO and Weston is the chief financial officer. We own eleven properties, in the upscale and midrange markets, mostly on the West Coast. Five years ago, I wanted the company to buy the Heartwood Inn. Didn't happen then, but now it's a go. For the next few months I'll be dividing my time between Heartwood and Seattle."

"Seattle?" She seemed to roll the word around in her head. "You're based in Seattle."

"Born there, grew up there. The company's there."

"And you have no desire to live anywhere else."

"You remembered."

She frowned. "Should I somehow have guessed Seattle five years ago?"

"I don't see how." He leaned closer, aching to touch her, but not feeling right about doing that yet. "I've been wanting to ask you…"

"Go ahead."

"Still writing books?"

She sat a little straighter. "You'd better believe it."

"Had any luck?"

"You mean, am I published?"

"I do."

"Yes, I am. I published my first and second books myself. They did well. For the third, I signed with a publisher. As of now, I'm working on my sixth book with them."

"So, eight in total, then?"

"Yes."

"Wow, Payton. You've been busy."

Her gaze shifted away. She bit the corner of her lip, just like she used to do when she hesitated to do or say whatever she had on her mind. "After the Larch Tree Lounge, I never took another crappy job. I figured I really needed to go for it with my books—put up or shut up, you know? I put in my time on the farm, and I wrote my books and, well, it's been working out."

A silence fell between them. She bit her lip again, looked away.

He leaned across the table toward her and lowered his voice to a near-whisper. "I suppose I should confess…"

She widened her eyes, faking alarm. "Nothing scary, I hope."

"Only a little. I've stalked you—your first name, anyway, because that's all I had. I searched for you on Amazon. I Googled the hell out of you and whenever I went into a bookstore, I would ask the clerk if he or she knew of any authors named Payton who wrote fantasy stories. When I admitted that I didn't know this wonderful author's last name, the clerk would patiently explain to me that there are a number of subgenres in fantasy fiction, and did I know which one this author named Payton No-Last-Name wrote in? I would admit I didn't have a clue and the clerk would then manage to come up with three or four fantasy authors whose first or last name was Payton. None of them was ever you."

"Fantasy is a pretty big section."

"You'd better believe it is. A guy could get lost in there."

"I write under P.K. Dahl," she said, her eyes sad, or maybe worried—but about what?

"Ah. I probably never would have found you that way, then."

"No—well, maybe. You might have spotted my headshot on the back of a dust jacket somewhere, I suppose."

The dark-haired woman appeared with their antipasto. She set it on the table between them and gave them each a plate. "Please enjoy."

"It looks wonderful," Easton said.

With a nod and a smile, the woman left.

He glanced at Payton. She stared at the oval serving dish piled high with cured meats, olives, pepperoncini, mushrooms, anchovies, artichoke hearts and various cheeses. She almost looked ill.

What the hell was going on with her? "Payton. What's the matter? You're not okay. Talk to me. What's bothering you? Are you feeling all right?"

*Feeling all right?*
No, she was not.
She had no idea where to start. No clue how

to do this. She kept telling herself to wait for the right moment. But there wasn't one. There never would be one.

"Payton." Easton sounded slightly frantic now. "What is it? What can I do?"

She dragged her gaze up from the untouched appetizer between them to meet his waiting eyes. "I… Oh, God…"

"What the…?" He started to rise.

She shot out a hand and grabbed his wrist. "No. Please. Just, um, don't get up. Stay there."

Slowly, he sank back to his seat. "Tell me what's going on."

She needed to do this. She needed to go ahead, to get it out. "Easton, I have to tell you something…" The words got all blocked up in her throat.

For some reason, she still had hold of his wrist. He turned his hand over and grabbed on to hers. His grip was so warm. Strong.

Five years had passed since that last time they'd said goodbye at the Heartwood Inn. She'd known him for one week. And still, she'd never stopped missing him—missing him while fearing that she'd never see him again, that she'd ruined everything with her rules. Memories of their time together swirled in her head. She wanted to cry.

She wanted to scream.

"Just tell me." He gave her hand a squeeze. "It's okay. Just say it, whatever it is."

Now his touch burned her. "Please. You need to let go."

He released her. She yanked her hand back to her side of the table.

"Sorry," he said. "I didn't mean to—"

"It's okay. It's nothing you did. It's…" She made herself say it, just blurted it out. "Easton, I, um, I had your babies."

The silence that followed seemed to go on forever.

Finally, a sound escaped him, something midway between a groan and a sigh. He sat back, hard, as though she'd shoved him in the chest. "What did you just say?"

She'd stopped breathing at some point. Her head spun—maybe from lack of oxygen. Maybe from sheer disbelief that this was finally happening. He was here. And she was doing a crap job of telling him about the boys.

Gulping in a giant breath of air, she nodded. "I got pregnant five years ago." She forced the truth out, fast. Frantic. "We have identical twins, boys, Penn and Bailey."

Easton had no words. Not a single one. He stared at the woman across from him. He knew his mouth was hanging open, but he couldn't summon the will to shut it. His ears rang.

This must be some weird dream he was having. It couldn't be real.

Her big eyes grew shiny. A tear dribbled down her soft cheek. She picked up the leather-bound book from the seat beside her. Gently, she laid the book on the table.

"I'm so, so sorry." Her voice came out broken sounding, all breathy and weak. "I did try to find you. I…" She pressed her lips together, squeezed her eyes shut and then opened them again. "Easton, just read this." She pushed the book toward him. And then she took her cell from her bag and typed out a text.

His phone beeped in his pocket.

"That's from me," she said. "It's my address at the farm. You're, um, welcome to come to breakfast tomorrow. You can meet the boys. We can talk…"

*Wait. What?* "The boys?" he asked stupidly. "Penn and…?"

"Bailey." She grabbed her bag and slid from the booth. "Just read it. We'll talk."

And then she started walking, headed for the door.

He should probably stop her, demand that she answer his questions. But his mind was blank as a bare white wall and his body sat frozen in place.

## Chapter Six

Sunday morning, Payton woke at a little after six. Her eyes felt grainy. She'd hardly slept at all.

The good news? She, Auntie M and Josie rotated responsibility for early-morning chores. Today wasn't her day. She could just lie in bed for a while, stare at the ceiling and try not to wonder if Easton had read her journal yet, if he believed that she would have moved heaven and earth to find him if only she'd known how.

She listened. Silence. Even anxious about Easton and worn-out from tossing and turning all night, she smiled a little, picturing the boys sound asleep upstairs, looking like the angels they weren't.

"Coffee," she whispered to no one. No point in lying here, really. She had way too much weighing on her mind to have the slightest hope of drifting back to sleep.

Not bothering to turn on the bedside light, she pushed back the covers and sat up. Shoving her feet in fuzzy slippers, she pulled a floppy cardigan over her flannel sleep pants and wrinkled T-shirt and headed for the kitchen. She had no idea what made her pause at the great room window that looked out on the front yard.

Beyond the porch, in the minimal light cast by the solar lamps that flanked the stone walk, she spotted the shiny SUV parked out in front. She could see the driver—or at least the shadowed shape of him—behind the wheel.

*Easton.* Who else could it be?

For several lengthy seconds, she just stood there, staring out at the dark outline of his head and shoulders, unable to move.

Absurd. She needed to snap out of it.

Okay, she'd made a mess of everything.

But there was nothing to do now but go out there and deal with the poor man.

She flipped on the porch light and went out the door.

He emerged from the car and crossed around in front of it. They met halfway up the walk.

He looked as haggard as she felt and his hair was all spiky, like he'd slept on it hard and then forgotten to comb it—hers probably looked about the same. She resisted the need to start madly combing her own tangled locks with her fingers as he said, "I want to meet them."

"Of course."

"And a DNA test. I want one of those. I'll set it up."

"Absolutely."

"I read the journal, some parts more than once. You're a hell of a writer and I can't believe all the ways we messed up. We messed up so bad."

Her throat felt tight, achy. She swallowed hard to relax it. "We had to have our stupid eight-nights-and-goodbye fantasy."

"Yeah."

"I know I already said it last night, but I'm so sorry, Easton. Just really, really sorry."

He put up a hand. "You don't have to keep apologizing."

"Yes, I do. I really do."

"We were both at fault."

She wrapped her old cardigan tighter around her. "When I left you that last time, you wanted to go ahead and exchange numbers, at least. I was the one who—"

"Don't," he said. "It's not important now."

"Yes. Yes, it is." Was she losing it? Sure felt like she was. Her eyes burned and no amount of blinking was going to hold the tears back.

"Hey." He reached out, hooked his big, warm hand around the back of her neck and pulled her against him. She surrendered to his embrace. It felt good, to have him there, to lean on him. He stroked her back. "We did what we did," he whispered. The too well remembered warmth of him, the scent of his skin, the solid, muscular shape of him—they broke her heart, made her want to throw back her head and wail for the loss of him, for all these years without him, for the impossibility of ever making things right for him. He'd lost four years of his fatherhood—more if you counted the months of her pregnancy, when he should have had the right to be there, to help out if he'd wanted to.

He said, "There's no going back and changing it now. What matters is what we do from here on out."

Sniffling and trying not to show it, she pulled away. "I know. You're right."

"Good. Because it's nobody's fault."

"I hear you. I do." She didn't agree with him, but what good would it do to keep beating him over the head with her greater culpability for the years that he'd lost?

None. She knew that.

Pulling a hair tie from the pocket of her sweater, she gathered her hair in her fist and anchored it up in a sloppy ponytail. "So." Squaring her shoulders, she forced a smile. "Coffee?"

"Please."

"This way."

Inside, she turned on some lights and led him

to the kitchen at the back of the main room. "Have a seat."

He glanced around the open space as he pulled out a chair at the table. "This is nice."

"Thanks. It's comfy." She went to the single-serve coffee maker and brewed him some French roast, filling the painful silence with talk about the house, explaining that when she got her advance on her first contract, she'd had the open, bare-beamed attic made into a big combination bedroom and playroom for the boys. "I put a bathroom up there, too. The second contract, I put in bamboo floors and redid both the kitchen and my combination bedroom and office. Next up, I'll take on the bathroom down here. I want a soaker tub and a walk-in shower with one of those rain heads." She set a full mug in front of him. "You just take it black, right?"

He looked up at her. Their eyes held. It all felt so strange and awful and wonderful at the same time, to have him here. In her kitchen.

"Black, yeah. Thanks," he said. The sound of his voice broke the spell that had held her locked in place, staring down into his eyes.

She went back to the counter and brewed a mug for herself. "I was thinking that, for a while, you should just be Easton to the boys. Give them time to know you a little before the whole 'this is your dad' conversation?"

"Till after the DNA, you mean?"

She turned and braced her hands back on the counter behind her. "Or maybe longer. I mean, we could decide together when the time is right."

His full mouth thinned. "How long, Payton?"

"A while. I don't know. I'm asking if we could please play it by ear."

"All right." He didn't sound happy. But at least he'd agreed to do it her way.

It hit her all over again, that he really was here, in her kitchen at Wild Rose Farm. It just felt so unreal. "Thank you."

He picked up the mug and had a sip. "About the journal you gave me. There were pages torn out."

The missing pages. Well, no surprise that he'd noticed their absence. She'd been unable to completely cut them away because of the binding. As a place to put words, paper was so unforgiving. She'd hoped, though, that he wouldn't mention the pages she'd removed.

So much for her hopes. "Sometimes, I would get self-indulgent. No reason you had to read any of that."

"But you wrote it to me."

"Yes, I did."

"So those things you call self-indulgent, they were meant for me."

"Yes, but I changed my mind about them, and so I took them out." She spoke firmly, with finality. He wasn't getting those pages and he needed to accept that.

And apparently, he did accept it. He said, "All right—but I have another question."

She suppressed a sigh. "Fair enough."

"You wrote it for me, and you've already cut out the parts you decided you didn't want me to see."

"Isn't that what I just said?"

"So then, it's mine. I can keep it."

His flat statement shocked her, somehow. She realized she hated to part with it permanently. That journal was a record in her own hand of her sons' first four years.

But she'd lived those years with them. He hadn't. And she never would have written it if not for him and her desperate wish that someday she would give it to him, that he would know his children. That he wouldn't end up like her own dad, who never knew his own child. "It's yours."

He looked at her so intently. But he only said, "Well, good, then. I just wanted to be sure. What time do they wake up?"

"Usually around seven, but probably earlier. They'll hear us and come down…"

Her coffee had finished brewing. She took her mug to the table and sat with him. He watched her, his eyes unreadable, as she sipped and swallowed.

"Are you hungry?" she asked.

"Coffee's fine for right now, thanks."

She pushed up out of her chair enough that she could look at the stove clock on the far side of the peninsula counter: 6:25. "This is silly." And awkward and painful and all kinds of difficult, sitting here, waiting for the sound of the boys stirring upstairs. "How about if I just go wake them up?"

He looked simultaneously panicked—and relieved. "Yeah, great. You want me to—"

"Go with me? No. For this first time, I'll just bring them down if that's okay."

He frowned. But then he nodded. "Fair enough."

God. This was hard. And awkward. And weird. Every smallest choice as to what to do next seemed weighted with outsized importance.

"You okay?" he asked cautiously, and she realized she was just sitting there, chewing her lip, wondering if they should be doing this a whole different way.

For five long years she'd feared that he would never meet his sons. Now it was actually happening, and she felt absolutely certain she must be doing it all wrong.

"I'm good," she lied. Rising, she headed for the stairs.

They came down five minutes later, Payton and two boys—the twins he'd seen at the market the day before.

One wore dinosaur pajamas and boot slippers printed with turtles. The other had spaceships flying on both his pj's and his slippers and carried an action figure in one hand. They were quiet, coming to a stop at the foot of the stairs and gazing at him through eyes the same color and shape as the ones he saw when he looked in the mirror— or at his brother, for that matter.

Payton herded them forward. "Boys, this is Easton."

"Hullo," they said, more or less in unison.

The one dressed in spaceships added, "I'm Penn and he's—"

"I'm Bailey," said the other boy, and giggled.

"Great to meet you," replied Easton. He was already cataloging certain tiny differences between the two. Penn had a left-side cowlick. So did Bailey, but his stuck out an inch farther up his head. Penn's hair was a slightly lighter brown than Bailey's. Both had dimples, but not in precisely the same spots.

"Mom said you're her friend." Penn seemed doubtful about that.

"Yes, I am." Hey, if he couldn't say *I'm your dad* yet, being Mom's friend would have to do. At one time, he'd been very friendly with Mom. And he fully intended to get friendly with her again. Soon. "Your mom and I have been friends for five years."

The two boys shared a glance, after which Bailey announced, "We're four."

Penn was still on the case of the stranger at the kitchen table. "Where have you been?" he demanded.

"I live in another town."

Penn frowned. He seemed unsure of what to say next.

Bailey had already moved on. "Mom, are we going to Auntie M's for breakfast?"

"Not this Sunday. Today I thought we would just go ahead and have our breakfast here. We can visit with Easton while we eat."

"Can we eat now?" asked Penn, suddenly much more enthused about breakfast than he was about some guy who'd shown up out of nowhere at six thirty in the morning and lived in another town.

"In a minute," she said to the boys and then offered Easton another cup of coffee.

"Only if you let me fix it. You?"

"Yeah, thanks."

Payton got busy serving the kids muesli with sliced bananas and almond milk and Easton dealt with the pod machine. The two kids ate with enthusiasm, shoveling cereal in their faces and whispering together.

Easton drank his coffee and tried not to stare at them in wonder. He found simply looking at them extremely disorienting, but mostly in a good way.

He kept thinking of the moment he'd first seen them at the market, how they'd reminded him of him and his twin. This morning, he saw how much they looked like him and his brother at that age. They were his. He had zero doubt of that now.

And that moment at the market kind of ate at him, the more he thought about it. What were they doing at that other booth with that farmer he'd assumed was their father?

Payton offered scrambled eggs and he accepted, at which point both boys decided they wanted eggs, too.

"They pretty much never stop eating," Payton explained with a rueful twist of her soft lips.

"We're big and strong." Bailey flexed his muscles.

Penn snatched up the action figure he'd set next to his cereal bowl and waved it around. "Incredible Hulks!" He let out a growling sound.

Payton bargained, "I'll need help."

There were no objections from the boys. They all pitched in, including Easton. After breakfast, the boys carried their plates and forks to the sink and then ran back upstairs.

Easton watched them go and wanted to follow.

At the sink, Payton chuckled. "You want to go with them?"

He hesitated. It seemed to be going pretty well, this first visit. But he didn't want to press his luck. "They hardly know me yet. Would they be all right with me just showing up in their room?"

She grabbed a towel printed with roosters from a hook by the sink and dried her hands. "Give me a minute and I'll go with you."

"That works, thanks."

He waited at the table as she took a left at the foot of the stairs.

A few minutes later, she reappeared in jeans and a bulky blue sweater, her hair freshly combed and loose on her shoulders. She gave him that smile of hers, the one he'd been missing for five long years. "Let's go."

They went up together to a bright, open space with big windows and the same bamboo floors as downstairs, half of it set up as a bedroom with two single beds, the other half as a play area. First off, the boys showed him their Halloween costumes. Bailey would be a Minion. Penn had chosen Edward Scissorhands. Easton learned they would attend a Halloween party that evening at a neighbor's barn, where they would hang out with other local kids, play games and win prizes.

"And get candy!" Bailey crowed in delight.

"Now let's play trucks," said Penn. He grabbed a toy tractor off a shelf. "Here, Easton. You get the tractor."

They ended up on the playroom floor, banging their trucks into each other and making crashing sounds. It seemed to be going pretty well, Easton thought. For the boys, at least. For him, well, the otherworldly feeling increased. Like his brain had gone on overload.

He had sons, sons he'd lost four years—five counting Payton's pregnancy. He should've been there for that, too. He'd missed too damn much. And he needed *not* to miss another minute. He already knew how it should go, where they should take it from here—where they *would* take it from here if he had anything to say about it.

He needed to get with Payton alone, ASAP, and get her agreement about what would come next.

She leaned close. "How're you doing?"

Penn let out a good imitation of a roaring engine and rammed Bailey's dump truck with a pickup. Bailey made crashing noises as he rammed Penn right back. Easton whispered not altogether truthfully, "I'm good."

"I'm going to leave you to it, then."

He felt a moment of panic but refused to let it take over. "I think I can handle it."

She gave him a teasing grin. "Come on down when you've had enough."

Payton left them as the boys attacked his tractor with gusto. They all three made crashing sounds.

A few minutes later, he heard voices downstairs.

"It's Auntie M and Josie!" announced Bailey. "Let's go down!" He and Penn dropped their vehicles and jumped to their feet.

Easton followed them down the stairs, where Payton introduced him to her aunt and her sister. Aunt Marilyn was tall and slim with short gray hair and a sweet smile. Her last name was Dunham. Josie—last name LeClaire—had dark eyes, light brown skin and acres of curly hair piled loosely on her head with a bow stuck in it. She wore overalls that accented her rounded belly.

The boys jumped around, showing off. Easton thought that both Aunt Marilyn and Payton's apparently pregnant sister seemed a little wary of him, but friendly enough.

"Okay, you two," Payton said to the twins, who were rolling on the floor, wrestling with each other the way Easton and Weston used to do when they were that age. "Settle."

The boys fell apart and lay there on the rug by the sofa, giggling and breathing hard. Easton kind of loved that they had no end of energy, yet also mostly tried to do what their mom told them to.

Marilyn went and stood over them. She braced her lean hands on her narrow hips. "I need help making brownies over at my house."

The boys scrambled up. "We'll go!" Penn volunteered.

Not two minutes later, Easton and Payton

had the house to themselves. They stood near the table, kind of eyeing each other. She offered more coffee.

He shook his head. Now he had her alone he had things he needed to say. "After I left your booth at the market yesterday, I saw the boys at another booth."

"Right. The Huckston Honey booth. Kyle Huckston is a longtime friend of mine. Sometimes, at the market, he takes the boys for a while—to give me a break, you know? Tom, the older man you probably saw in the Huckston booth, is Kyle's dad. Tom's a real sweetheart, but he'll talk your ear off if you give him half a chance."

Easton felt anger rising. "I thought the younger guy at the honey booth—Kyle, you said?"

"That's right. Kyle."

Where had he heard that name before? "Wait a minute. Kyle. The first guy you ever had sex with. *That* Kyle?"

She folded her arms across her chest and gave him the evil eye. "I don't know whether to be touched that you remember some small, intimate detail of my life that I shared with you five years ago—or pissed off that you have the nerve to give me attitude right now."

She had a point.

But he wasn't feeling all that rational at the moment. "Just answer the damn question. Is the

Kyle I saw yesterday the same one you told me about five years ago?"

"Yes," she said, her voice flat and her expression scarily calm. "They are one and the same—and tell me, Easton, how many women have you been with in the past five years?"

"I... What does that have to do with any of this?"

"So you haven't been with anyone? You've lived like a monk, pining for me?"

"What are you getting at?"

She only continued to face off against him, her beautiful eyes arctic, her mouth a flat line.

He scoffed. "We're talking about that Kyle guy and suddenly you need to know if I've dated anyone since the night you walked out of my room for the last time?"

"Yeah. That was my question. Are you going to answer it?"

He considered a flat refusal. But then he gave in. "I tried, okay?"

"You tried what, exactly?"

"To see other people, to meet someone else."

"And...?"

"I went out more than once. It never amounted to anything."

"Well, I tried, too. With Kyle. And it didn't work out."

He did not like the sound of that. "What do you mean, you *tried* with him?"

"Last year, he asked me to marry him. I said yes."

He wanted to break something—maybe pick up one of the chairs at the table and throw it across the room. But he held it together by a thread. "What happened?"

She took a minute to answer, her breathing slow. Carefully controlled. "We both realized it wasn't going to work, that we didn't have the right kind of love to be married. We broke it off by mutual agreement."

"But he's still hanging around you."

"No. He's not 'hanging around.' He's my friend. Always was. I hope he always will be."

His anger spiking again, Easton muttered a few choice words under his breath. "Yesterday, I thought he was their dad." He could hear the fury in his voice and knew he was being a dick about this, trying to put blame on her, make her the bad guy here.

Her eyes accused him. "What are you getting at, Easton?"

"When I found you at the market, they were right there, Bailey and Penn, right there three or four booths over from yours, right there with your 'longtime friend' and former fiancé, the first guy you ever slept with."

She leaned toward him, chin out, ready for a fight. "You just hold on a minute—"

"No. *You* hold on." He should shut his damn mouth. He knew that. But he didn't. "I have a question for you, Payton. Why is your former fiancé watching my sons at the market?"

"You're being a complete ass," she remarked much too softly.

"It's a simple question. Just answer it."

"I already did. Because he's my friend. I've known Kyle *and* his parents my whole life. I don't remember a time when I didn't know them. Kyle and I used to play together when we were still in diapers. He loves Penn and Bailey. It's as simple as that." She bit her lip. Glanced away.

"But you were *engaged* to him." The words came out ragged, scraped off the back of his throat.

"Yeah, I was. And it didn't work out, but Kyle and I kept our friendship. That's a *good* thing. I'm *glad* about that."

Easton no longer wanted to throw a chair. Now he wanted to hit something—or someone. Preferably, the beekeeper.

And he should let it go. She hadn't married the guy and was no longer engaged to him. That was answer enough and he really needed to get a grip on himself. He was out of line here and even he knew it. But somehow, he couldn't hold the next question inside. "Why did you change your mind about marrying him?"

She still had her arms folded tightly over those fine breasts of hers. "I don't owe you an explanation about what happened between me and Kyle. You left here and I couldn't find you and we'd agreed, anyway, that we were both moving on. I had every right to marry Kyle if I'd wanted to."

She did, absolutely. And jumping all over her was no way to get the answers he sought. He tried to speak gently. "Please. Just tell me."

For a moment she said nothing. She tipped her head to the side and studied his face. Finally, with a hard sigh, she explained, "I love Kyle, but not in the way a woman should love the man she marries. I realized that and so did he. That's all there was to it. But as I said, Kyle's a good guy and we are still friends."

"I see."

"Do you?"

"Yeah." He ground his teeth together and made himself apologize. "I'm sorry. This is hard and I seem to be screwing it up royally."

She chuckled, the sound without humor. "You're right about that—and now you've at least apologized, I will share with you that Kyle has a girlfriend now. Her name is Olga Balanchuk and she's a barista at one of the coffee places here in town. I like her a lot and she's crazy about Kyle. He feels the same about her."

Now Easton felt like a first-class ass. Probably because he'd just behaved like one. "Uh, well that's great. For Kyle. And, er, Olga, too, I'm sure."

"And as for my trying to get rid of you yesterday, yes. I was. I wanted a chance to speak with you alone before you met the boys. Is that so unreasonable?"

"No. It's not. It was the best way to handle it."

"So why all the attitude?"

"I, uh…" He shut his eyes, shook his head. "Look. I found you at the market after spending years telling myself to give it up, that I needed to move on and stop feeling like someday I'd see you again. And then, there you were. I found you and I was so damn happy. You have no idea. I was walking on a cloud, but also telling myself to keep a lid on it, take it one step at a time. I was thinking we'd go to dinner, catch up a little, see what maybe came next…"

She looked at him, unspeaking, for several seconds. He had no idea what might be going through her head.

And then she yanked out a chair and dropped into it. "Have a seat." She gestured at the next chair over.

He didn't know what else to do with himself right then, so he sat down.

Neither of them said a word for at least another minute. Maybe two. Outside he heard a dog bark. Farther off, a rooster crowed.

About then, she reached over and put her hand on his. Her touch caused all manner of havoc in-inside him. He wished that they could just sit here like this forever, her hand on his, staring into each other's eyes.

He turned his hand over, so they were palm to palm and then he twined their fingers together. That felt even better.

"You don't have to explain," she said. "I get it. I do."

"But I want to explain. I was just so glad to see you. And then I find out I'm a dad. I've got two boys and they really like this Kyle guy and you almost married him." He put his other hand over their joined ones. "It's a lot. I'm not dealing as well as I should."

"And that is completely understandable," she said quietly.

He winced. "I hate that I'm making this even more weird than it already is."

"You're not. I mean, you're suddenly a dad. You've got to be reeling."

"Pretty much, yeah—and I do know already that those boys are mine."

"Yes, they are." She spoke carefully, as though navigating a conversational minefield. She also pulled her hand free of his hold. He let it go with great reluctance. "And I appreciate that you believe me. But really, you don't have any way of knowing for certain that they're yours. That's why it's great we can do DNA."

"Payton. DNA is good. I'm just saying that I don't need it to know I'm their dad."

She didn't disagree in words, but it was written all over her face.

"Let me show you." He pulled out his phone, logged on to Facebook and went to his mother's timeline, where she posted no end of photos of him and his brother from infancy to their thirty-third birthday dinner two weeks ago. He found a picture from way back when—him and Weston with their bikes in front of the family house in Washington Park. "We were maybe five here, West and me." He turned the phone so that she could see.

"Wow," she said softly. "That's… Yeah. It could be Penn and Bailey—I see that."

He set the phone on the table. "So for me, the test is kind of a formality."

"It's important," she insisted. "That you have it. You understand that, right?"

"Yeah. I'll arrange for the test tomorrow and let you know."

"That works."

He wanted to take her hand again. It had felt so

right to have her fingers woven with his. Looking at her now, *he* felt right—righter than he had since the night they said goodbye. She'd walked out of his room and his life and for a long time, he'd feared he would never see her again. He never should have let her go that night. When he came back the first time, he should have kept looking, not just accepted what Midge Shanahan told him. What if Payton had married the damn beekeeper, for God's sake?

But she hadn't. And he'd finally come back a second time. He'd come back and he'd found her, and he wouldn't lose her again.

He'd gotten everything wrong till now. First, he'd married the wrong woman, then he let the right one get away—with his babies, no less. And the one chance he'd had of finding her before his children were born was stolen because he'd believed a heartless stranger who'd lied right to his face and said Payton was already married.

"Easton?" Payton leaned closer. He looked into her eyes again. He saw worry in them. But then a smile trembled across that sweet mouth of hers. "Thought I'd lost you there for a minute. You seemed a million miles away."

"Yeah. I was thinking…"

"About what?"

"I was thinking that I never got you out of my mind. You were always there, in my head, in my heart. I didn't trust what we had, and I lost you. And dear God, I have missed you."

She made a sound, low. Mournful. "I missed you, too."

"The boys matter," he said. "The boys are everything. But I think, even if they weren't in the picture, I would still want you, Payton, still be in love with you."

Her eyes went impossibly wide. "In love with me?"

Okay, that was maybe a little too much at this point. But did he want to take it back? Hell, no. "That is what I said."

"I... Easton, I think we have to slow down a little here."

"Why? It's true. I'm in love with you. I've been in love with you for five long years."

She put up a hand. "Stop. Really. We can't—"

"But we *can*. You know we can. I just need you to tell me if there's a chance you could love me, too."

"It's not that simple. We hardly know each other."

Not true. He did know her. In eight nights and those two magical days at that B and B in Hood River, he'd come to know all he needed to know, everything that mattered.

Hadn't he?

She looked at him through worried eyes.

Fine. Maybe he should dial it back a little. Somehow, around her, that both-feet-on-the-ground guy he'd always considered himself flew right out the window. "So then, you don't feel the same—or you don't trust what you feel?"

"I don't, um…"

"Yeah?"

"I don't trust what I feel. I can't. It's too dangerous. I'm not…good at relationships. I've never really made one work. Mostly, I avoid commitments, you know?"

Gently, he reminded her, "You love your aunt and your sisters. You seem pretty damn committed to them."

"Well, yes. They're my family. We take care of each other. I'm there for them and they know they can count on me."

"And what about our sons? Raising children is the biggest commitment there is and you went for it—you took it on."

"Yeah. Of course I'm committed to Bailey and Penn."

"And from what I've seen so far, you're an amazing mother."

She blushed. It was the cutest thing. "Thank you."

"It's true." And he might as well just say it, just let her know where he stood, what he wanted most of all. "I want to marry you, Payton. That's what I want, for us to be a family—you, me and Penn and Bailey."

She swallowed, hard. And then she whispered, "You have to see. We don't really know each other. We had a week. It was a fling."

"I know what I feel. I think that you feel the same."

"Easton, you're not hearing me. I don't even know you, not really."

"Who are you trying to convince right now? I don't think it's me. You're scared. You're just scared."

Her chair scraped the floor as she jumped up. "This is way out there. You know that, right?"

"I disagree. Us getting married is the best option. It makes sense. We're a family, you, me and the boys. I only want us to start living like one."

"But we're not *that* kind of family." She zipped around behind the chair, putting it between them, and then gripped the back of it with white-knuckled hands. "I'm their mother and you're their father. We'll need to figure out how that's going to work, yes. But we can't get ahead of ourselves. First, we need the DNA test and then we can start talking about what comes next."

He wanted to get up, put his arms around her and promise her that everything would be all right. But he had a very strong feeling she might lose it completely if he so much as touched her right now. He stayed in his seat.

She went on, "I realize this is a complete shock to you, and I hate that you've been a dad for four years and didn't know it. It's clear that you want to make things right. I appreciate that. But as for getting married, well, no. Just no."

He gritted his teeth and made a conscious effort to ask quietly, "Will you please agree to think about it?"

*Think about it?*

Payton didn't want to freak the guy out any more than she already had. But really, he had no right to spring marriage on her at a time like this. Probably not ever.

How clear could she make it? True, she'd never forgotten him—and not only because he was the father of her sons. Their time together had been a perfect romantic fantasy. She had so many wonderful memories of all they'd shared in that brief, beautiful week. She would always treasure those memories.

But that week wasn't real life. He had to know that. Didn't he?

Judging by the focused way he looked at her and the determined set to his sculpted jaw, apparently not.

If marriage were an answer to all the big questions, she would have gone ahead and married Kyle. Kyle knew her so well and she knew him. Their lifestyles matched and he lived right here in the hometown where she planned to stay. Okay, he wasn't the boys' biological father, but he'd wanted to be their dad and they adored him.

But she hadn't married Kyle. She'd known it wasn't right with Kyle and he had, too, in the end.

Now, for completely different reasons, it wasn't right with Easton, either.

He sat there looking so much like the man she remembered, the man she wanted to drag out of that chair and straight to her bedroom—though she would do no such thing. They had so much to consider, so many important decisions to tackle now. They had two children to raise and they lived in two different states. All that would need to be dealt with. She needed to stop thinking how much she wanted to climb him like a tree. They had a thousand things to work out and complicating that with sex…?

Uh-uh. She had to be wiser, more focused that that.

As for arguing further now, that would get them nowhere. She needed to keep it civil between them even more than she longed to shake a finger at him and deliver a lecture concerning all the reasons the two of them getting married was not a solution to anything.

*But he says he's in love with me!* squealed the needy little girl within her—the one who never met her father, the one whose mother treated her as little more than an inconvenience.

*Of course he would say that he loves you*, she sternly reminded her own inner child. *He's a good man who wants to do what's right.*

Easton tried again. "Look. All I'm asking is that you consider it."

"Consider it…"

"Yes. Just think about marrying me."

Well, that wasn't what she would call a tough ask. Of course she would think about it. How could she *stop* thinking about it? He was her dream lover come true. She'd given birth to his children—and why not be honest, with herself, at least. She still had a mad crush on him.

"Just think about it," he coaxed again.

"Okay, Easton." Her voice sounded absurdly breathless. "I will consider your, er, proposal."

## Chapter Seven

The next day, Easton called the family law firm in Seattle. They recommended a reputable company in Portland that did legal DNA testing. The company set everything up and arranged for Easton, Payton and the boys to have their cheeks swabbed at the hospital in Hood River. Easton went in on Tuesday. Payton texted him Wednesday to let him know she and the boys had given their samples that day.

Easton considered going out to Wild Rose Farm that afternoon. But he didn't. He was buried in work at the inn. Then on Thursday, he flew to Seattle in the morning for meetings, returning to Heartwood that night.

Friday morning, the DNA results became available online.

As soon as he saw them, he called Payton from his office trailer at the inn. "It's official," he announced when she answered the phone. "I'm a dad."

She laughed. "Congratulations."

"Thank you. I'm sending you the link and the password. You can see for yourself."

"It's not necessary. I know already that you're the boys' dad."

"Well, I mean, just in case you don't believe me…"

"Wait." She laughed again, the sound husky and sweet. "Isn't that my line?"

"You think?"

"Easton, stop teasing me."

"Uh-uh. Teasing you is too much fun." And it seemed like forever since Sunday. The past few days, he'd not only been busy with work, but he'd also been giving her some space, reining in his need to be with her and the boys. Well, enough with the reining in. "I want to see them." *And you…*

"Of course." Her voice had gone all-business. "And we should try to come to an agreement, you and me, about the next step."

*The next step…*

A wedding—*their* wedding. That sounded like a great step to him. But he'd accepted that getting a yes from her would take time. Luckily, he would be in Heartwood a lot over the next several months.

"We could talk tonight. I'll pick you up. I tried out that steak place around the corner from Barone's and it's pretty good." He waited for her response. When he got nothing but dead air, he gave her a little nudge. "So, then. Jerry's Grill?"

"I would need a sitter. It's kind of short notice."

"Maybe your aunt or your sister is available…?"

He heard her draw in a slow breath and he knew he was about to get shot down. But then she said, "All right. I'll figure something out. I'll meet you at Jerry's. Six thirty all right?"

He shouldn't push. "Let me pick you up."

"Easton…"

"I was thinking that I could maybe see the boys, just to say hi."

Another hesitation, and then, "All right. Pick me up."

*Yes!* He fist-pumped like a twelve-year-old, swung his feet up onto his desk and leaned back in his swivel chair. "I'll make the reservation for seven and be there at your place at six fifteen."

"Works for me."

He hung up feeling like a million bucks—make that a billion.

And then he called his brother. "Are you sitting down?"

"Should I be?"

"Do it."

"Done."

"I found Payton."

"How? Where?"

Easton gave him the short version of what had happened at the farmer's market the Saturday before, adding, "And that's not all."

"Wait a minute. You found the mysterious Payton six days ago and you never said a word to me till now."

"I wasn't ready to get into it."

"You did seem distracted yesterday…"

In Seattle, they'd been in two meetings together and then gone out to grab something to eat. "I had a lot on my mind."

"Let me guess. You already got down on one knee."

"Yeah, well. I'm working on that. The woman will not be rushed."

"Good for her."

"Hey. You're on *my* side, remember?"

"Yes, I am. And marriage isn't something you should be rushing into."

"Says my wild younger brother who tends to make rushing into things a way of life—and truthfully, I'm not rushing into this. I've waited five lonely, endless years for her. I'll keep waiting as long as she needs that. But I don't have to *like* waiting. Especially not considering the situation."

"There's a situation?"

"A big one. You still sitting down?"

"I am. Why?"

"Payton has twin sons, identicals, like us. Bailey and Penn are four years old."

Weston drew an audible breath. "Yours?"

"They are. I knew it the minute I laid eyes on them. You'll see what I mean when you meet them. But Payton insisted that I arrange for DNA tests."

"It is a good idea."

"I know. As I said, I set it up. The results came in this morning. Those boys are mine."

Now Weston chuckled. He knew how much Easton wanted kids. "Two boys. Congratulations."

"Thanks. I hate that I've missed four years of their lives. And Payton's pretty strong-minded. I'll have a lot of convincing to do, getting a ring on her finger and all four of us living together in Seattle. But still. I'm happy. Really happy."

"You share the news with Mom and Dad yet?"

"Not yet. I want to talk to Payton first, invite her and the boys to visit Seattle for the weekend."

"You already sound like an old married man—having to check in with the wife first."

"That's how it works."

"You do sound happy. And I'm happy for you, man."

That night, when Easton knocked on Payton's door, Josie answered. She greeted him warmly and ushered him in as both boys came running down the stairs so fast, it was a miracle they didn't end up tumbling to the floor.

"Easton!"

"Hi!"

"Hey, guys." He tried hard not to sound like he felt—desperate to know them, to be a real part of their lives. "Good to see you."

They both started talking at once, about how they'd been promised popcorn and a movie with Josie. *"Minions!"* Penn fist-pumped for emphasis. "And we get to stay up!" he cried with sheer glee.

"Maybe until *nine*," declared Bailey, looking awestruck at the thought.

"If you want, you can watch *Minions* with us," offered Penn.

What Easton wanted was to grab them both and hug them tight. But he had to remember that sudden hugs from some guy they'd met exactly twice might be considered a little inappropriate.

And that pissed him off. He needed to move forward with this. He wanted his kids and he wanted Payton and he wanted them now.

Penn bargained, "If you stay, you can have popcorn, too."

"Not tonight." Payton came through the door on the far side of the stairs. She wore a silky black shirt and a tan skirt with tall suede boots. Easton wanted to sweep her into his arms and kiss every inch of her—yet another important goal that would have to wait. "Take Easton upstairs," she said to the boys. "Show him what you built today."

"We built a trike!" Bailey grabbed his hand. Easton looked down at those small fingers in his and felt weak in the knees.

"Come on!" Penn commanded. He led the way, with Bailey pulling Easton along behind him.

A kid-size plastic tricycle made of interconnected tubes with thick black wheels waited in the middle of the play area. Bailey climbed on and rode it in a circle as Penn explained that Aunt Josie and their mom had helped them put it together.

After Bailey, Penn took a turn. When he got off, Bailey regretfully announced that Easton might be "a little too heavy" to ride.

"Sorry, Easton." Penn pooched out his lower lip in sympathy.

Easton reassured them that he didn't mind. He asked them what else they'd done that day. They explained that they went to preschool until lunchtime and came home to chicken noodle soup, a half sandwich and a cookie each.

He stared at them in wonder as they chattered away about their Fire 7 kid tablets and how they'd already used up their screen time for the day. "But we still get to watch the movie with Aunt Josie," Penn explained.

"Because sometimes a little extra screen time is okay," Bailey clarified.

"Next time you come see us," said Penn, "we can show you *Teach Your Monster to Read*. It's fun and very educational."

"I can't wait," he replied, and meant it.

Payton, who'd pulled on a coat, appeared in the open doorway to the stairs. "Ready?"

They all four trooped back to the lower floor. After a flurry of goodbyes, he and Payton went out into the chilly October night. The ride to the restaurant went by mostly in silence. He had so much to say to her and he didn't know where to start.

At Jerry's, where they got a booth as cozy as the one they'd shared at Barone's, Easton kept reminding himself to take it slow with her, to enjoy the moment, let things unfold naturally. They chatted about his work and hers.

"I bought one of your books," he said. *"Emperor of Falling Stars."*

"Did you read it?" she asked with a cagey little smile.

He held her gaze. "Is this a test?"

That smile bloomed wider. He had to actively resist the need to crane across the table, wrap his hand around the back of her neck, pull her close and crash his mouth down on hers.

"Easton?"

"Hmm?"

"Did you read it?"

"Every word." Right now, his days were packed. He was up at five and didn't get back to the rental house until eight or nine at night. Every night since he'd left her house Sunday, he'd wanted to call her. But he'd restrained himself. Reading something she'd written had made him feel closer to her. "I liked the battle scenes best."

"Spoken like a true guy."

"Hey. They were exciting. You had me believing in dragons with knives beneath their scales and giant bats with golden wings."

"Thank you." Was she blushing?

Yeah, definitely. Blushing. It was a great look on her. "The sex scenes were pretty hot, too."

"I, um, do my best."

Their food came. She asked how the work was going at the Heartwood Inn.

He had a sip of wine. "What can I tell you? There are meetings and more meetings. Working lunches. Dinners, too. My office is a trailer on-site. Yesterday, I flew back and forth from Seattle for more meetings I couldn't afford to miss."

"Well, I have to say I think a major redo is a great thing. Make my day and tell me you're eighty-sixing all the plaid."

"Yes, we are. And also the log cabin look. We're going for a sleeker sort of rustic."

"I like the sound of that—and you mentioned that you rebrand your properties. Gotta admit it makes me a little sad to think there will be no more Heartwood Inn in Heartwood."

"Don't be sad." He resisted the urge to put his hand over hers. "We're keeping the name."

That mouth he needed to kiss immediately widened in a big smile. "I'm so glad to hear it."

And come on. Wasn't that enough chitchat?

Yeah, okay. He'd promised himself he would take it slow.

But they had important matters to discuss.

She tipped her head to the side, kind of studying him. "You've got that look."

He set down his wineglass. "Which one is that?"

"You've got something to say, Easton. Just go ahead. Say it."

"All right, I will. I not only read your book. I read that journal. Over and over. I keep thinking of all the time we've wasted, the time we should have been together. I want you. I want my kids. I'm trying to keep a lid on myself, not to rush you. But five years in the dark, not knowing what was happening with you, with them—having no damn idea there even *was* a them. Missing so many firsts, not there to help out, not there to walk the floor when one of them got sick… Look, the truth is, I've always wanted kids."

She made low, sad little sound. "Yeah?"

"Yeah. Sometimes, the past couple years, I found myself thinking that might never happen for me. And now I learn that it happened four years ago, and I didn't even know. I just don't want to waste any more time I could be spending with them. *And* with you."

"I don't know what to say to that."

*Say yes. Marry me. Let's get going on the rest of our lives.* Somehow, he kept those words from flying out of his mouth. He knew that he needed *not* to keep pushing her, to give her time to say yes to him.

But then she shook her head and said, "I don't want to leave my home, Easton. My sister's having a baby on her own and my aunt, who raised me, is not getting any younger. It's kind of my turn to be there for both of them."

What could he say to that? "I do understand."

"So, are you planning to move to Heartwood, then?"

No, he was not. But hope had flared inside him, anyway. She hadn't said no. And she'd clearly been thinking about it—about the two of them and the boys making a family together. "I would move if I could."

She leveled a long, cool look on him. "So what you're saying is you can't, and you won't."

He didn't see how, not and keep the job he

loved. He needed to make his mark in the family company. He wanted to build on what his father had created, to pass it on to the next generation feeling proud of his contribution. "The company is in Seattle. I need to be there a lot—that's all I'm saying."

"Got it. And my life is here." She sounded pretty dug in.

But he refused to get discouraged. Somehow, some way, they would work it out. "Well, there is good news."

She looked at him over the rim of her wineglass. "Tell me."

"I *am* here the majority of the time until the first of the year, at least, to get the Heartwood Inn expansion and reno off the ground."

"And then?"

"By mid-January, the project should be on track and I'll be based in Seattle again."

"Well, that's good."

"That I'm leaving in January?" He meant it as a joke—partly, anyway. At the same time, he couldn't help thinking that if he didn't change her mind by January, what next?

Would she agree to a long-distance relationship for a while? How would it work out, with the boys? Would he see them on weekends and for a few weeks in the summer? No.

Just no. He refused to start thinking of a life

where his kids and the woman he wanted more than anything didn't live with him full-time.

The warm color in her cheeks had intensified. "I'm glad you're here, Easton. And we do have some time to work it all out." She looked at him so earnestly. His spirits lifted a little as she continued, "We can be together often while you're in town. You can see the boys on a regular basis, I hope, and get to know them better..."

That didn't sound so bad. "So then, you have been thinking about it, haven't you? Thinking about you, me and the boys—about a possible future together?"

"Yes," she said, her voice quiet but firm. "Yes, I have."

Payton touched her glass to his. They drank.

She couldn't stop staring at him. Unbelievable, after years of missing him, to have him right here across the table from her.

It had been so long since she'd left his room at the Heartwood Inn that final time. Until he'd appeared at the market a week ago, she'd kind of given up on ever finding him. She'd schooled herself to accept reality, come to grips with the fact that she would never see his face again. Her dreams of running into him one day felt way more like fantasies than anything that might really happen.

But now, here he was—and she needed to stop lying to herself about what was going on here. About how much he meant to her.

Most of her adult life she'd sworn she would never marry—that marriage was an antiquated custom unnecessary in a world where, with a little help from friends and family, a woman could earn her own money, take care of her own business and raise her children herself.

She loved, trusted and counted on Josie and Auntie M—and Alex, too, though her eldest sister didn't come home nearly often enough.

Payton had a great life. She'd created the career she'd always wanted. Her children, whom she'd never actually intended to produce, had turned out to be the best thing that ever happened to her. She'd told herself she had it all, and mostly, she'd meant it. Yet still, something had been missing. Her days of flings and casual hookups were behind her. She'd wanted more. Her life felt lonely without the right man to share it with.

So no, she was not entirely averse to the idea of marriage. Hadn't she almost tried it with Kyle? Luckily for her, she'd figured out in time that she couldn't marry just any wonderful guy. It had to be the *right* guy.

And yeah, to her, the right guy would very likely always and forever be the one sitting across from her now.

For him, she could almost see herself tackling happily-ever-after. She'd never really gotten over him and her boys were his, too. It seemed wrong to call it love at this point, but it could be. If only they took the time to let love grow.

"You're not talking." A teasing smile tugged at the corner of that mouth she hadn't kissed in five endless years.

She understood that she needed to make herself clear to him. "I just want to take it slow, okay? We can see how it goes, but with no prearranged outcome."

"Yes."

She couldn't help chuckling. "You sure you don't need at least a few seconds to think it over?"

"I'm sure. And I have a request."

Of course he did. She ate a bite of steak. "I'm listening."

"I want to fly you and the boys to Seattle. I want you to meet my family."

She set down her knife and fork. "What part of 'we're taking it slow' wasn't clear to you?"

"I got that part."

"And yet suddenly we're flying to Seattle with the boys? Easton, it's too soon. We need some time. You can get to know your sons, let them get to know you. Then we'll tell the boys you're their dad. And *then* we can start planning a meeting with your family."

"What if it was just the two of us for the first trip?"

"Easton, the whole point is not to rush."

"Rush? There's been no rushing. My sons are four years old."

"You keep saying that."

"Because it's true. We have two children to-gether. You and I *will* be in each other's lives. I've met your sister and your aunt. I've even met that guy you almost married. I hope to meet your other sister sometime soon. My parents are grandpar-ents, and they don't even know it."

She poked at a roasted brussels sprout with her fork. "When you put it that way, I really feel like a jerk."

"You're not a jerk."

She gave the brussels sprout another poke. "Yeah, well, I'm not so sure about that."

He reached across and stilled her hand, send-ing shivers of heat up sliding her arm. "Leave that poor little brussels sprout alone."

"Oh, Easton. I'm trying to get this right."

He set his napkin on the table, slid out of the booth and back in on her side. "You're doing great." His big, warm arm encircled her, and he pulled her close.

She gave in and leaned against him. It felt so good, the warmth of his body, the clean, spicy scent of him that she remembered so well. His lips brushed the crown of her head and she wished they could just sit here, the two of them, nice and close, their bodies touching, his arm across her shoulders, for a year. Or ten.

He whispered, "Let me arrange a visit. We'll fly up, just you and me, for the weekend."

"I haven't even asked you how much you've told them."

"I told Weston everything. He's looking forward to meeting you and excited to get to know Penn and Bailey."

"And your parents?"

"I haven't said a word to them yet, about you or about the boys. Come to Seattle with me. We'll tell them together. A family dinner, you, me, Weston and my mom and dad."

"That's a little bit scary."

"No. It won't be. They're going to love you and I think you'll like them, too."

"So, just like that, over dinner, we lay it on them that they have two grandsons?"

"Essentially, yes."

"I don't know. Say it doesn't go well, say they don't like me and—"

"Of course they'll like you."

"I hope so. But just say that they don't and then we hit them with the news about Penn and Bailey and they flip out and—"

"Hey. It's going to be fine. But I'll tell you

what. We won't say anything until you're ready. Not until dessert."

"Right. Because dessert is the perfect time to tell your parents they have grandchildren."

"No, because dessert is the end of the meal and by then you'll know if you're comfortable telling them about the boys."

"And if I'm not? I mean, they still need to know at some point, right?"

"I'm just saying that if you don't feel comfortable some reason, if you want me to speak with them first or you want more time to figure out *how* to tell them, then we won't say anything right then and we'll reevaluate what comes next."

"Are you saying I'm supposed to give you a signal that it's okay to tell them?"

"Payton. Don't you think we'll both know if it's going well?"

She sipped her wine. "You're right. I'm sure we'll get the feeling either way."

"So then, we're agreed. A trip to Seattle and dinner with Weston and the 'rents."

She still felt way too on edge about it. But she did want to meet his family. And they needed to know about the boys. "We're agreed."

His arm around her shoulders tightened. "Excellent."

She tipped her head back to look in his eyes.

Her heart ached, but in a good way, to have him right here with her, now. At last. After so long apart. "Oh, Easton. I have missed you for such a long, long time."

He lifted his other hand and cradled her throat in his palm the way he used to do forever ago. His long fingers brushed under her hair, caressing the sides of her neck, almost reaching her nape. A soft moan escaped her as his touch set off sparks of desire. Her breasts ached for his mouth. Her core flared with heat.

"Payton," he said again. Only that. Just her name. And it was everything, all the promises never made. All the days and nights without him.

"Too long," she whispered.

"It's felt like forever," he agreed, his mouth bent close, his breath warm on her skin, scented with wine.

Their lips met—light as a breeze at first. But only at first. The sparks between them burst into flame. The kiss went deep and thrillingly hot—and so right. His kiss was just right. His mouth felt made for her.

*Our first kiss in five years…*

It seemed a miracle. It certainly felt like one, a deep, slow, searingly intimate miracle.

Easton, holding her close.

Easton, right here with her at last, his mouth fused to hers.

"Finally," he said low and rough as he lifted his mouth from hers.

She reached up, laid her hand on the side of his face and shivered a little at the slight scrape of stubble against her palm. "We'd better behave."

He reached across the table and pulled his plate in front of him, followed by his wine, and his napkin, too. "Finish your dinner. You'll need the energy."

They went to the house he'd rented. He took her coat and then led her straight to his bedroom.

"I can't stay long," she warned as he unbuttoned her shirt and eased it off her shoulders. "I need to get back…" The last word ended on a groan because he'd bent to bite her nipple through the white lace of her pretty bra—and yeah, she'd worn nice underwear tonight.

Almost as if she'd hoped this might happen…

"Don't rush me." He continued to torment her breast with his hot mouth as he unzipped her skirt and pushed it down, taking her satin panties with it.

The skirt dropped to the floor easily enough, but her panties got hung up on her boots. When that happened, he bent and swung her up on his shoulder in a fireman's carry.

"Easton!"

"Shh." He gave her a playful slap on her bare butt.

She slapped him right back.

"Here we go." He put her down on the bed and knelt to unzip her boots and take them away.

In only her bra and argyle socks, she leaned back on her hands. "You're much too busy taking off *my* clothes."

He ripped off a sock. "I have my priorities in order."

She grabbed his shoulders and gave him a push. "Get naked. Stop fooling around."

She took off her other sock and her bra as he stripped down to nothing in no time at all.

"Come here." She meant it as a command, but it came out a plea.

"Right here." He joined her on the wide bed and gathered her into his big, hard arms. In the light from the lamp by the bed, his eyes were so dark, deep as oceans. "Payton…" He stroked her hair away from her forehead. "Here you are. In my bed. Finally…"

And then he kissed her, guiding her down to the mattress as his lips held hers. The kiss was endless. Her hands were everywhere. She needed to touch every inch of him.

How could this be possible? That he was here. In her arms. At last.

His mouth left hers. Before she could cry out at the loss of his kiss, he began kissing his way down her throat to her bare breasts, where he lingered for the sweetest stretch of time as she speared her fingers in his thick, wavy hair and pulled him tighter, harder, closer.

There was no such thing as close enough.

On down he went, dipping his tongue into her navel on the way, pausing at her lower belly to explore the faint white lines there. "New," he whispered, and traced one with his tongue. "From the boys?"

She cradled his gorgeous face between her hands and nodded down at him. Her eyes felt hot, wet from happiness and yearning all swirled around together. To be here, again, like this.

With him.

"I never thought we would be like this," she whispered. "I thought you were lost to me. I thought our sons would never get a chance to know you. I thought this—you and me, naked together—I thought it would never happen again."

He bit her stomach, a slow, deliberate scrape of white teeth on her willing flesh. She moaned. He reached up and touched her mouth. She sucked his fingers inside, nipping at them, sliding her tongue around them.

"Payton…" He stole his wet fingers back, dragging them down the middle of her body as his clever mouth moved lower. She opened her thighs wider to accommodate his shoulders.

And then he was there, at the core of her, spreading her open for his fingers and his tongue.

She lost track of the real world. There was only his touch, the way he played her body, his fingers stroking, his tongue teasing, arousing, luring her, drawing her toward the peak with such passionate skill.

He could have made her climax swiftly, but he drew it out the way he used to do, making her beg for it, slowing down more than once as she almost hit the brink, easing her back from the peak each time.

"Not fair," she objected.

He only chuckled and renewed his efforts to drive her higher and hotter than before.

When she finally went over, she screamed his name. He kept his mouth on her, making it last, making her beg him never, ever to stop.

After that, as she lay limp, he kissed his way up her body and gathered her to him. They rested, whispering together, laughing, skin on skin at last after so long apart.

It wasn't long before she reached down between them and wrapped her fingers around him, going up on her knees so she could take him in her mouth, teasing him at first, with her tongue and her stroking fingers, then sinking down, taking him all the way to the back of her throat.

"Wait," he commanded, gruff and low.

She glanced up and saw he held a condom between his fingers. "Uh-uh." Even with her mouth full of him, she managed a shake of her head.

He held her gaze. "Payton." It came out on a groan. "I need to be inside you. I need you now."

Her whole body melted at that look in his eyes. She gave in. Lifting away from him and sitting back on her knees, she watched as he rolled the condom down over his thick, hard length.

He reached for her. Pulling her close, he rolled her beneath him. Eager and so very ready, she wrapped her arms and legs around him. He claimed her willing body in one deep, hard glide.

She moaned at the sheer rightness of it, to be with him again this way.

At last.

With a sigh of complete surrender, Payton shut her eyes and let the pleasure sweep her away.

## Chapter Eight

"I hate to ask," Payton began sheepishly.

It was nine thirty Friday night. Bailey and Penn were sound asleep upstairs. One week had passed since the DNA results came in and Payton had gone out to dinner with Easton to introduce the important subject of a parenting plan—and ended up not only naked in his bed until 3:00 a.m. Saturday, but also agreeing to fly with him to Seattle to meet his brother and his parents.

"You hate to ask what?" Auntie M sipped her Full Sail Amber Ale as she and Josie shared a look. They both seemed to be trying not to grin. On the floor at Josie's feet, Tinkerbell's tags jingled as she scratched behind her ear.

"Wait." Josie squinted at Payton as though hoping to see inside her head. "Let me guess. You and the baby daddy have decided to elope. You want us to watch the boys while you're gone."

"No problem," said Auntie M with one of her sweet little smiles. "Of course we'll watch my great-nephews." Then she gave Josie's arm a playful slap. "And Easton's a good guy. I like him. The boys are all over him whenever he drops by—which has been just about every day this past week. Payton's obviously in love with him. Calling him a baby daddy is disrespectful."

Payton put up a hand. "Hold on a minute." Last Friday night had been beautiful. But since then, she'd put serious effort into keeping a lid on her unquenchable desire for the father of her children. She and Easton had a lot to work out and going at it like rabbits only confused the issue. "I did not at any time say that I'm in love with Easton."

"As if you had to say it," Aunt Marilyn chided. "And why are you defensive about it? Love is a beautiful thing."

"I never said I'm in love—nor am I defensive."

"She said, defensively." Josie snickered. Payton gave her a slap on the other arm. "Ow! Why is everybody slapping me?"

"Girls. Be nice," Auntie M admonished, her expression annoyingly angelic.

Josie drank from her mug of pregnancy-safe herbal tea. "I like Easton, too. And it's not disrespectful to call him what he is."

Auntie M frowned. "But isn't a baby daddy usually irresponsible? I would not in any way call Easton irresponsible. It's hardly his fault that he and Payton made some ridiculous agreement never to see each other again and—"

"Yoo-hoo!" Payton raised her hand, like a kid in class. "There is something I really need to talk to you guys about."

"We're listening," replied Josie.

"Whatever we can do, sweetie." Aunt Marilyn enjoyed another sip of her ale.

"Easton's asked me to fly up to Seattle with him this coming Thursday to meet his parents and his brother. I'll be back Sunday. I know it's a big ask, but I don't think it's time yet to bring the boys along and I was hoping that maybe—"

"It is not a big 'ask,' as you put it," Marilyn cut in. "I would love to look after Penn and Bailey while you're gone."

"What Auntie M said." Josie folded her hands on the bulge of her six-months-pregnant belly. "It's no trouble."

"Go." Auntie M made a shooing motion. "Meet the in-laws."

"They're not my in-laws," Payton reminded her aunt patiently.

"No yet." Marilyn bestowed another of her beatific smiles.

"I really don't know what's going to happen, so can we not go predicting some fairy-tale ending, please." She aimed a stern look at her aunt and then at Josie, too.

Marilyn put up both hands. "So shoot me. I'm sixty-five years old. I lost your uncle John twenty-five years ago. That is one long dry spell. Forgive me if I can't stop myself from living vicariously through my nieces."

Josie snort-laughed. "We both know you're not living vicariously through *me*."

"Find a man to love, Josephine." Aunt Marilyn leaned over and kissed Josie's cheek. "Make your old auntie happy."

"Make yourself happy," Josie advised. "Get on the apps."

"Maybe I don't need the apps." Auntie M smiled, slowly and very sweetly.

Josie peered at her more closely. "Wait a minute. Let me guess. Ernesto asked you out."

"We're friends," replied Auntie M, still wearing that sly smile.

Currently visiting from the Salinas area, where he owned an artichoke farm, Ernesto Bezzini was a lifelong friend of Tom Huckston's. A few days ago, Ernesto had shown up with Tom and Kyle to cut down a hundred-foot Douglas fir twenty feet from one of the barns. The tree had rotted clear through the base.

"Friends already," Payton teased.

"I do like him," Aunt Marilyn replied sweetly. "He stopped by for a visit yesterday evening and he's taking me to dinner tomorrow night."

Josie pushed her chair back and went to pour

more hot water over her teabag. "Nothing like romance in bloom."

"We're *friends*," Auntie M. insisted.

"He's a hot silver fox and you like him a lot."

"Pshaw." Marilyn turned to Payton. "So we're set. You're off to Seattle Thursday and we'll look after the kids."

"Thank you."

Josie sat down again. "You're biting your lip, Paytaytochip. Stop. It's going to be great. The future in-laws will love you and the kids will be fine here at home with us."


"An air taxi. Who knew?" Payton joked once they were in the air on the way from Columbia Gorge Regional Airport to Sea-Tac. It was just the pilot, copilot, Easton and Payton in the small plane that really kind of did look like the cab of a car from inside.

"Gets me there in an hour," he said. "To drive takes three to four times that long and flying from PDX is just as bad, time-wise, once you add in the drive to Portland and airport security."

"Because busy hotel tycoons need to get where they're going fast."

"Don't mock me. It's true."

"I can't wait to see your place. I'll bet it's super fancy…"

Super fancy, indeed.

# Loyal Readers
# FREE BOOKS Voucher

## We're giving away

**THOUSANDS**

**of**

**FREE**

**BOOKS**

**Romance**

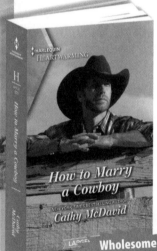

**Wholesome Romance**

**Don't Miss Out! Send for Your Free Books Today!**

# Get up to 4
# FREE FABULOUS BOOKS
## You Love!

To thank you for being a loyal reader we'd like to send you up to 4 FREE BOOKS, absolutely free.

Just write "YES" on the Loyal Reader Voucher and we'll send you up to 4 Free Books and Free Mystery Gifts, altogether worth over $20, as a way of saying thank you for being a loyal reader.

Try **Harlequin® Special Edition** books featuring comfort and strength in the support of loved ones and enjoying the journey no matter what life throws your way.

Try **Harlequin® Heartwarming™ Larger-Print** books featuring uplifting stories where the bonds of friendship, family and community unite.

Or **TRY BOTH!**

We are so glad you love the books as much as we do and can't wait to send you great new books.

So don't miss out, return your Loyal Reader Voucher Today!

*Pam Powers*

# LOYAL READER
# FREE BOOKS VOUCHER

**YES! I Love Reading, please send me up to 4 FREE BOOKS and Free Mystery Gifts from the series I select.**

Just write in "YES" on the dotted line below then return this card today and we'll send your free books & gifts asap!

➡ YES ⬅

Which do you prefer?

☐ **Harlequin® Special Edition** 235/335 HDL GRGZ

☐ **Harlequin Heartwarming® Larger-Print** 161/361 HDL GRGZ

☐ **BOTH** 235/335 & 161/361 HDL GRHD

| FIRST NAME | LAST NAME |
|---|---|

ADDRESS

| APT.# | CITY |
|---|---|

| STATE/PROV. | ZIP/POSTAL CODE |
|---|---|

EMAIL ☐ Please check this box if you would like to receive newsletters and promotional emails from Harlequin Enterprises ULC and its affiliates. You can unsubscribe anytime.

SE/HW-820-LR21

Easton's house was four thousand square feet on three levels right on the waterfront in the northwest Seattle neighborhood of Ballard. He had three enormous bedrooms, each with its own luxurious bath.

She probably should have objected when he carried her small suitcase directly to the top-floor primary suite, but she felt nervous and excited—about the trip, about meeting his family. She didn't really want to sleep alone in a strange bed.

Or at least, that was her excuse du jour.

She stood at the wall of windows looking out on Salmon Bay, wondering how she'd gotten here with this man she'd really only known for a matter of weeks total, who just happened to be her sons' long-lost dad.

He put his big, warm hands on her shoulders.

She resisted the need to lean back against. "It's beautiful here," she said.

"You look good here." He bent close. His lips grazed the side of her neck, sending tingles of pleasure zipping all through her.

"I'm nervous about meeting your family."

He turned her to face him and tipped up her chin. "Don't be. They're eager to get to know you."

"Wait. We said we would…"

He put a finger to her lips. "They don't know about Penn and Bailey. We'll tell them together, as we agreed."

"Do you think it would maybe be better if you talked to them first?"

He just looked at her. Tenderly. Patiently.

"Okay." She let herself breathe again. "I guess it doesn't really matter. I would be on edge no matter how we'd decided to go about this."

"Weston's still a bachelor. I'm divorced. My mother and father really want grandchildren. Lately, my mother has started complaining that if my brother and I don't get busy, she'll never be a grandma. They're going to love you. And when they find out about the twins, they'll be thrilled."

"Yeah?"

"Yeah."

"I wish we were just going to get it over with tonight." The meet-the-parents dinner was tomorrow night.

"If you're that anxious, I can call them, see if…"

Now she was the one covering his lips with her fingertips. "No. Don't listen to me. Tomorrow is great. Fine. Perfect."

"You're sure?"

"Yeah. Nervous. But sure."

He touched the side of her face, his fingers straying over her left cheek as he guided her unbound hair back over her shoulder. "You need a distraction."

She saw what would happen next right there in those gorgeous sea-blue eyes. "Oh, my, my..."

"What?"

"You. This. Everything."

A worried frown creased his brow. "Are you okay?"

"I will be." She eased her fingers around the back of his neck and pulled him down, so their lips were a breath's distance apart. "I just need you to kiss me..."

Two hours later, they went out for seafood. Back at his gorgeous house, they talked about streaming a movie, but ended up in his big bed doing what came naturally.

They didn't get to sleep until two in the morning. Before they drifted off, she reminded him that this was a special circumstance, the two of them, in his bed together. "When we get home, we really need to keep our hands off each other."

He nuzzled the side of her throat the way he liked to do—the way she loved him to do. "Refresh my memory. Why?"

"It's important. To keep the focus on what matters."

"You matter." He nipped at her jaw. "Marry me. Then we can keep the focus our family. Together. Problem solved."

"A long-distance marriage? I don't think so."

He rolled to his back and pulled her in close to

his side. "Stop worrying. It's all going to come out just right. Shut your eyes. Get some sleep…"

The next day, Easton had meetings. Payton fiddled around on her social media in the morning, consulted for a while with her assistant, called the farm at noon and spoke to the boys and then to Josie and to Marilyn. Both her sister and her aunt reassured her that all was well.

Later, she took a walk around Easton's trendy neighborhood, visiting two indie bookstores, where she chatted up the booksellers, signed instock copies of her books and said she would love to do a signing when her next book came out. She gave the owners her card.

Back at the house on Seaview Drive, she showered and put on the flared black knee-length asymmetric skirt, short-sleeved cobalt blue cashmere sweater and matching high-heel suede pumps she'd carefully chosen for tonight. The outfit looked fine, she thought—but was fine good enough? Why hadn't she brought an alternative or two?

"Because you would only hate all three of them," she informed her scowling face in the walk-in closet's full-length mirror.

"Who are you talking to in here?" Easton stood in the open doorway.

She went to him and wrapped her arms around

his neck. "None of your business. How was your day, honey?"

"Tedious." He kissed her. "You look gorgeous."

She stepped back, grasped the frilled hem of her skirt in both hands and curtsied. "Thank you."

"I need a quick shower and we're out of here."

Joyce and Myron Wright's beautiful gray-shingled Dutch Colonial sat at the top of a winding cobbled walk on a broad, tree-lined street in the heart of Washington Park.

"Nice place to grow up," Payton remarked as they went up the walk to the deep, inviting front porch.

The carved mahogany door swung open just as they reached it. A pretty older woman with a short blond bob and a giant smile greeted them. "You're here! Come in, come in..." She stepped back and they entered a foyer, beyond which was a white living room with coffered ceilings and tall windows looking out on mature trees and lush plantings. This year, fall had come late. The trees still had their leaves, many resplendent in the colors of autumn lit beautifully by in-ground and overhead lights.

"Hello," said the tall, graying man who stood a few feet behind the blonde woman. "I'm Myron."

"I'm Joyce!" the woman announced excitedly.

"And you are Payton. So good to meet you." She turned to Easton. "Son…"

"Hey, Mom." He hugged her.

"Come on in," said the other man, Easton's twin. The two were as identical as Bailey and Penn, though Weston had longer hair and a certain devilish glint in his eyes.

"Take off your coats," said Myron, "and let's get comfortable in the living room."

A few minutes later, they all sat around the giant fireplace, where a cheery fire burned. Myron served drinks as they shared getting-to-know-you chitchat.

Payton found herself relaxing. Joyce and Myron were nice people. They seemed thrilled that Easton had brought a girlfriend home. As for Weston, Payton liked him, too. Easton's twin had a wicked sense of humor and he seemed as genuine as his brother—yet not quite so preppy somehow, and definitely more easygoing. A beautiful family, she thought.

Eventually, they moved into the dining room off the enormous chef-worthy kitchen. It was all going beautifully. Payton could laugh at herself now for ever being anxious about this meeting.

Myron said he hoped to get Payton and Easton out on the new boat he'd bought. "We can make a day of it," he said, "have a picnic on the water."

Joyce said how pleased she was that Easton

had found someone special. "I swear, Payton. In the past few years, I've wondered if either of the boys will ever—"

"Mom," Easton warned.

Weston backed him up. "East's right, Mom. Don't go there."

Joyce laughed and her husband patted her hand. "Well," she said. "I am glad you're here, Payton. I'll leave it at that."

Myron said, "I understand you help run the family farm and also write books…?"

She slid a glance at Easton. "What have you been telling them?"

"Not enough." Joyce sent her older son a reproachful glance. "Just that he met you five years ago and ran into you again when he started the Heartwood Inn project—and about your family's farm and that you're a writer."

"And how glad he was to see you again," added Myron.

Joyce beamed. "Yes—though we would have guessed that, anyway. He hasn't brought anyone special to meet us in years."

Pleased that the dinner seemed to be going so well, Payton told them about growing up in Heartwood and a little about her writing.

Joyce said, "Myron and I have kept promising ourselves we would get down there to look around. He wants to buy a motor home, can you believe it, one with all the bells and whistles. He wants to take his time, see America."

"Why not?" Myron sipped his coffee. "We've been all over the world. Now we need a long, leisurely tour of the good, old US of A."

"Including Oregon," said Joyce. "I know the Hood River area is beautiful. And then there's Easton's near obsession with the Heartwood Inn." She wore a coy little smile. "Somehow it all makes sense now. It was always more than some run-down log cabin hotel he found so fascinating…"

Easton was having a great time.

He shared a grin with his brother. West raised his glass of Macallan 18 in a silent toast.

It was going well. And it felt damn good, to be here in the house where he grew up with the family he loved and the unforgettable woman he'd once given up hope of finding again.

But he *had* found her. And she seemed to be hitting it off just fine with his parents. It was all going to work out; he knew it now. Eventually, he would convince her to marry him. In time, she would agree to move with the boys to Seattle.

Tonight, he could almost forgive himself for losing her because of some silly agreement he should have had sense enough to break before he let her disappear from his life. Yeah, he'd blown it then.

But this time, they would get it right.

They would have it all. Love and a good, full life with their children around them.

When they finished the rack of lamb, his mom served coffee and a strawberry cream tart.

As he and Payton had agreed, he waited until they'd settled in over the dessert to make the big announcement.

"Your favorite," said his mom as she set a big slice of tart in front of him.

"Looks so good, Mom."

She patted his shoulder and moved on to Payton. "I hope you like it."

Payton beamed up at her. "It looks beautiful, thank you."

His mom moved on around the table and Easton sent a quick, questioning glance at the woman beside him. She answered with a glowing smile and a dip of her pretty chin.

Yeah. She was good with it. It was a go.

He waited until his mother settled back into her chair before speaking. "Mom. Dad." He held out his hand to Payton. She took it, her eyes shining in anticipation of what he would say next. "It just so happens that Payton and I have a surprise for you tonight."

His mother chuckled. Her cheeks were flushed. She must be expecting him to announce that he'd proposed, and Payton had said yes.

*Sorry, Mom. She hasn't given me a yes yet. But she will, and soon.*

His mom sent his dad a triumphant glance.

His dad said, "We do love surprises."

"Good." And Easton went for it. "Because, as it turns out, I not only found Payton again after five long years, but I also found my twin sons."

His mother gasped. "Wait. You're saying there's a baby?"

"Two boys, Mom. Twins."

Joyce sent a stunned glance at his father, who just sat there, looking startled. "Wait. But you haven't seen Payton in five years, you said."

Payton spoke up. "I got pregnant when Easton and I were together five years ago. Our sons, Penn and Bailey, are four years old."

"We've done the DNA test and it's official," Easton said. "Wait till you meet them. You will love them on sight. They look just like West and me, back in the day."

"But, Easton. Please. You can't be serious." His mother sent his father a frantic look. "Myron. This makes no sense at all to me." Her gaze swung back to Easton. "You said you 'ran into' her again by accident at an outdoor market."

"I did. I dropped in at the Heartwood Saturday Market and there she was."

"I don't..." His mother sent another swift glance at his father. She seemed...completely pissed off all of a sudden, which made zero sense to Easton. "What is going on?" she demanded.

His dad just blinked and shook his head.

It was like some weird nightmare. Things had been going beautifully, and then, out of nowhere, it all veered off the rails. They were suddenly headed straight for disaster. "Mom, Dad? What's the matter? I don't get it."

His mother shook her head slowly. "Well, Easton, we have to ask. How do you *really* know those children are yours?"

"I told you. DNA testing."

About then, Payton eased her hand free of his grip. He tried to grab it back.

"No," she insisted in a near whisper, her face suddenly pale. She lifted her chin and said to his mother, "I know it's kind of confusing. But five years ago when Easton and I met, we made an agreement not to exchange personal information. Neither of us wanted anything serious at the time. We had agreed that when he left Heartwood, that would be it. We would go our separate ways. But then later, after he was gone, when I found out I was pregnant, I had no way to get in touch with him…"

His mother stared at Payton coldly, with a look that judged her as it simultaneously dismissed her. "Oh, I'm sure."

"What the hell, Mom?" Easton demanded.

"What's happened? Why are you behaving like this?"

His mother glared at him. "Please, Easton. DNA can easily be faked. After what happened with Weston, you ought to know that."

West groaned. "Come on, Mom. It's not the same. East's been in love with Payton for five years. She's no Naomi."

*Naomi.* Easton saw the problem now. It had never occurred to him that he needed to factor in that train wreck with Naomi...

"Not the same as what?" Payton demanded. "Who is Naomi?" She looked completely confused and absolutely miserable now.

He held her unhappy gaze and willed her to understand. "It's a misunderstanding."

"Of what?"

"It's a long story, but I'd forgotten all about Naomi. I should have considered what happened with her. But I promise, it's going to be okay."

Payton scoffed. "Easton. It is not okay. Not in the least. And I still don't have the faintest idea what is going on here."

"Oh, you hadn't heard?" his mother piped up. "Six years ago Naomi Page, a girlfriend of Weston's, claimed she was having his baby. She faked the DNA proof and did it convincingly, all supposedly legal, everything aboveboard. We all believed that she was having Weston's child. She would have taken him straight to the cleaners if the real father hadn't spoken up at the last possible minute—at the altar, no less. Weston called off the wedding and arranged for another test. Turned out he was not that baby's father. Naomi Page was just some gold digger out to make a buck."

Payton drew in a shaky breath and swung her gaze to Easton again. Her eyes accused him. "You never told me about that."

"I'm sorry. It didn't even occur to me. I didn't think it mattered. It was years ago. And it was West, not me."

"Sorry, Payton," West put in ruefully. "I used to get up to a lot of crazy stuff back then. East's always been the steady, dependable one. Everyone knows it." He glared at their mother. "Mom. You're wrong about this."

"Every man can be duped." Their mother's voice dripped scorn.

Easton whirled on her. "You are behaving so badly. It's unacceptable. You need to stop."

"*I'm* behaving badly?" She flung out a hand in Payton's direction. "She's the one who's trying to extort you. I'm just trying to get you to see the light."

Payton gasped. Her cheeks flushed deep red and then paled.

Easton wanted to slap his own mother. "You have it all wrong, Mom, and you're saying things you can never take back. How many ways can I tell you *I* set up the test? I told Payton where to take the boys to get swabbed. That's it. That's all she did. She and the boys showed up where I told her to go and let a nurse take samples. I did everything else. At no point could Payton have manipulated the results."

"We'll need another test," his mother said self-righteously.

"Mom. I called *our* lawyers, Destin and Ericson. They recommended the lab. It was a strict chain of custody all the way."

His mother sent a furious glance at his father. "Myron. Do something. He is not listening."

His dad said, "Easton, your mother and I would like to speak with you alone."

Fat chance. "You have to be kidding me. Hell, no. Mom's on a rant and we all know it." He leveled a hard look at his mother. "I love you. I know you're a damn mama grizzly when you get some idea in your head that someone's screwing one of us over, but you'd better dial it back. Because you're wrong. You're off base in the worst way and I don't even know what to say to you."

His mother had her nose in the air. "Another DNA test. Your father and I will arrange for it this time."

He stood. "Forget it." He looked down at Payton. "God. I'm so sorry. Let's go." Payton shoved back her chair. "Come on," he said, and reached for her hand again.

But she shook her head. "Look. Your parents want to speak with you privately. You need to talk to them."

"No, I don't. Right now, I don't give a damn what they want or what they think they have to say."

"Well, I do. I refuse to be the bad guy here. I'm not getting in the middle of this." Now she was the one grabbing him. He let her pull him away from the table. Once she had him in the corner of the room, she took her hand off his arm and whispered, "You and I have no commitment as a couple."

He felt like she'd just hauled off and punched him in the face. "Payton. Come on. You know that's not true." He tried—again—to reach for her.

She put up both hands. "Don't!"

His dad said, "Let her go, son. We do need to speak privately."

Easton ignored him. "Payton, please—"

"You just don't get it," she hissed, leaning in close to him again, for his ears alone. "Talk to them. I'll be in the other room." She started walking.

He wanted to chase after her. But he knew she'd only order him to get back here and deal with his parents, both of whom he would gladly strangle about now.

Easton cast a glance at his twin. He didn't need to say a word.

West was already on his feet. "Payton. Hold up. I'll go with you."

When Payton entered the formal living room, she almost kept on walking. She wanted to grab her coat and her purse from the entry closet and march right out the door.

But Easton's brother said, "Have a seat."

She paused in midstep. "I don't know, Weston…"

He gently took her arm and guided her to a wing chair. "Sit."

"Fine." She took the chair.

"A stiff drink is very much needed in this situation," he said. "What'll you have?"

"It doesn't matter."

"Vodka tonic?"

"Sure. God, what a complete balls-up." Weston fixed her drink and brought it to her. "Thanks." She took a big gulp.

He poured himself another Scotch and took the other wing chair. "Sorry about my mother. She's mostly great."

"Until she's not?"

"In her defense, the thing with Naomi was

pretty traumatizing for her. Mom got really invested. She was so excited about having her first grandchild. She fought with my father when he suggested early on that we needed another test to be sure. They didn't speak for weeks. And Naomi was working Mom the whole time, kissing up one minute, the next threatening to disappear and never let them see their supposed grandchild again. Talk about a screwed-up deal…"

"I'm sure it was traumatizing for everyone," she muttered.

"Yeah, it pretty much was."

She hit him with the salient question. "So then why didn't Easton see this coming?"

"Payton, it was a long time ago. He's not me and you are not Naomi—believe me, you are nothing like her. Naomi really was out to get all she could get. You're not that. Not in any way. Easton *wants* a future with you. There's no comparison."

"Apparently, to your mother, there is."

As if on cue, the murmur of voices in the other room got louder. Joyce practically shouted, "Please. Maybe she has a friend at that hospital. She made a deal with that nurse who took the samples. You don't know what she might have done."

"I do know," Easton argued. "*She* insisted on the test."

"Of course she did. That's part of her game.

And why did she wait five years to tell you—and if those children *are* yours, how do you know she didn't get pregnant on purpose?"

"I told you." Easton sounded like he'd reached the end of a very short rope. "Put on your listening ears, Mom. Payton did not try to get pregnant on purpose. And she had no way to find me after I left Heartwood. She didn't know who I was."

"And why is that? You must not have been all that important to each other if you didn't even bother to exchange phone numbers before saying goodbye."

"Stop it, Mom. That we didn't exchange numbers was a *mistake*."

"Or maybe you just didn't care."

"I did care. And your logic is seriously flawed. You think she magically set me up and then waited patiently for five years for me to come and find her to give her all my money? Can't you see how ridiculous that is?"

Payton took another big gulp of her drink. It didn't help. She had to get out of here. Now. She took her phone from her pocket and brought up the Uber app.

"Payton." Weston sounded worried. "What are you doing?"

"Just texting a friend," she lied as she ordered a car.

In the other room, the battle raged. Joyce accused, "You've proposed already, haven't you?"

"Of course I have. I want to marry her. I've been missing her for five damn years, and we have two sons. She's the one for me."

"She's got you feeling obligated."

"Mom. You have no idea what you're talking about." He said something else, but more quietly so that Payton couldn't quite make out the words.

"I knew it!" crowed Joyce. "You've been taken for a ride. We're going to need to call the lawyer right away, get a *real* DNA test—and an ironclad prenup if you insist on going through with this..."

Weston cringed.

Payton had to stifle a burst of furious laughter. "I know, I know. She's a wonderful woman, right?"

"She *will* come around," Easton's brother promised sheepishly.

Payton stuck her phone back in the pocket of her skirt, set her drink on the side table and stood. "I'm leaving. Do not say a word to anyone in the other room."

"But Payton—"

"Stop talking." When Weston clamped his mouth shut, she went on, "I appreciate your efforts to make me feel better. You seem like a great guy, but I've had enough. My Uber's out front and you'd better just sit there and drink your Scotch until I'm gone."

Payton could still hear the voices in the dining room as she started walking. Not once glancing back, pausing in the foyer only long enough to grab her purse and coat, she went out the front door.

## Chapter Nine

Not two minutes after her Uber driver turned the corner and left Joyce and Myron's tree-lined street behind, her cell rang. It was Easton. She let it go to voice mail. He texted three times and called four more before she even got to Sea-Tac.

Once at the airport, she turned the phone off while she found a flight to Portland. She got one—the last flight out at 10:55 p.m.

Would Easton assume that she'd headed for the airport? She really didn't want to get into it with him right now.

She had hours till the plane took off, but she went on through security to her gate, anyway. And then she sat there at the gate, waiting, half-afraid he'd buy a ticket just to get to her before she could take off.

And equally afraid that he wouldn't. She wanted him to come after her—but she didn't want to see him right now.

Really, she was a mess. She turned on her phone again. Ignoring the cascade of call, text and voice mail alerts, she called Josie at home.

Somehow, she managed not to burst into tears at the sound of her sister's voice.

Josie knew immediately that something wasn't right. "What's happened? What's wrong?"

"I don't want to go into it now. Are the boys still up?"

"They just went to bed. Do you need to talk to them?"

She longed to hear their voices. "No. Let them be. I'll be home soon."

"What do you need? Where are you?"

"I'm at Sea-Tac. I've got the last flight out to Portland tonight."

"Easton." Josie said his name like a curse. "What did he do?"

"Did he call there?"

"No." It occurred to Payton at that moment that he probably would—as soon as he realized Payton had no intention of answering his texts or accepting his calls. "Did he get your number?"

"I didn't give it to him. But he can call the land-line for the farm and get Auntie M."

"I don't want him bothering her." Payton realized she would have to deal with him whether she felt up to that or not. "I'll take care of it. Don't worry."

"Are you sure you're all right?"

"I'll survive. I'm getting into PDX at 11:45 to-night."

"I'll be there to pick you up."

"No, Josie. You've got the boys. I'll get an Uber."

"All the way to the farm from Portland?"

"It'll be fine."

"Call Alex. She's right there in town and she'll bring you home."

"Josie. I don't want to bother her for this."

"Call Alex, or I'm coming to get you."

"All right, all right. I'll call Alex."

"Thank you. Now tell me. What did Easton do?"

Payton thought of Joyce, so nice at first and then so awful. A headache had started to pound behind her eyes. "I'll tell you all about it when I get back. Promise. Now, I've got to go."

"Call me. For anything."

"I love you. See you tonight or maybe tomorrow."

As soon as she got off the call with Josie, she sent Easton a text.

I'm fine. I don't want to talk right now. I'm just going to go home.

No sooner had she sent it off than her phone rang in her hand. No way was she answering that. She punched out another text.

Easton. I DO NOT WANT TO TALK.

Maybe the shouty caps would get through to him. But no.

Payton. Please. Where are you? Let me come pick you up.

No. We can talk tomorrow. I'll call you in the afternoon. Do not bother anyone at the farm.

Define bother.

Don't call them. I'll be home by tomorrow at the latest. As I said, we can talk then.

I'm at my house. Your stuff is still here. Don't run off. We'll work this out. Let me come pick you up.

This was going nowhere. She almost turned off the phone right then. But she sent one more text first.

Turning my phone off. Talk tomorrow. Good night.

Alex was waiting at the curb when Payton exited the terminal at PDX. Payton pulled open the passenger door and slid into the quiet comfort of the Audi hybrid SUV.

"Hey." Alex reached across the console for a hug. "Are you okay, Paytay?"

Breathing in Alex's familiar scent of Dune by Christian Dior, Payton hugged her sister tighter. "You've got to stop calling me Paytay. I'm a famous author with two children, much too mature to be called baby names."

Her sister squeezed her harder. "You'll always be Paytaytochip to me, baby girl."

"Ugh. But as for your question, I'll survive, thank you. I'm sad and angry and miserable and I just want to go home."

They sat back in their separate seats and Alex asked, "Right now?"

"Well, as soon as possible."

"No problem." Alex put the car in gear. "I threw some stuff in a bag and I'm ready to head for the farm—no suitcase?"

"Nope. I just walked out the door of his parents' house and had the Uber guy take me straight to the airport."

Alex eased the SUV forward. That time of night it was pretty quiet. A minute later, they were sailing along Airport Way. Not long after, Alex merged onto I-205.

Payton stared out at the road ahead, the darkness cut by their headlights and punctuated by bright pools of light mounted on wide green guide signs. "I really could have just called an Uber."

Alex laughed her husky laugh. "Are you kidding? This is a favor you're doing me. I don't get home often enough and we both know it."

"Right. Then you're welcome. I think."

"We'll be home in an hour. Time enough for you to tell big sister all about it…"

So Payton told Alex everything, from the complete surprise of Easton's return to their growing closeness over the past few weeks, to the awful way everything had crashed and burned that night at his parents' house.

"I swear, Alex, his mother turned on me so fast." She shivered. "One minute she's thrilled that Easton's brought someone special home to meet the family—and the next, she's calling me a gold digger and demanding another paternity test."

Alex sent her a sympathetic glance. "Sorry, honey. It sounds really awful."

"It was." She flopped back against the seat and closed her eyes. "It's probably for the best, though. Easton's been relentless, insisting that he wants us to get married, that he has to live in Seattle, but somehow we'll work it out, even though I've told him I'm not leaving Josie and Auntie M."

"You feel that he's not listening?"

"I wouldn't say that. It's just that I need time and space to agree to something as serious as marriage—even before you factor in my reluctance to leave the farm."

"But…?"

"But I've been weakening, you know. Leaning into what he wants, thinking the kids and I could maybe at least come home for most of the summer and whenever Josie and Auntie M need me, that Easton could join us whenever possible. That I could make it happen, be here in Oregon to work the booth at the market, come down and pitch in at weddings, manage the website sales and the spring and harvest tours."

The Hood River Fruit Loop tour included thirty farms now. Visitors from all over the country could take the tour, get the full experience of local farms and wineries. They could pick their own produce while enjoying the beauty of the Hood River area.

As for weddings at the farm, two years before, she and Josie had fixed up one of the barns and started renting it out for events. "Harvest time would be the worst," Payton said, "with all that goes on here and the kids in school up there. But there would be plenty of money. I could just fly home anytime something comes up. I could be flexible…"

Alex sent her a sympathetic glance. "And now you're thinking none of that would work?"

"More like seeing that I was jumping the gun. It's way too soon to be talking marriage—and after tonight, I kind of wonder if it could ever work at all."

* * *

It was one in the morning when Alex pulled the Audi to a stop in the graveled parking area on one side of Payton's cottage.

"The boys are at Josie's for the night," Payton said. "You get the upstairs to yourself."

"Well, I was just thinking—"

"Stop. You are not driving back to Portland tonight—correction. This morning. You wouldn't get home until after three."

"But I—"

"No buts, Alex. It's Saturday."

"I can get a lot done on a Saturday," Alex muttered defensively. "The office is quiet. There are no interruptions."

"Well, this Saturday, Kauffman, Judd and Tisdale will have to do without you. You're taking a little family time. Your sister needs you. At the very least, you're getting a few hours' sleep and staying for breakfast with Josie and me, your adorable nephews and your wonderful Auntie M."

Inside, Payton got her sister settled upstairs. After a good-night hug, she went on down to her room, where she got ready for bed, climbed in under the covers—and did some serious ceiling staring.

What she didn't do was turn on her phone. If she scrolled through Easton's texts and listened to his voice mails, she would never get to sleep.

Around two, the wind came up. It started raining. She listened to the sound of the wind howling under the eaves and the rain pinging on the window near her bed as she stared at the ceiling some more.

At a little after three, she heard a vehicle drive up outside and had zero doubt who that might be. Putting on her slippers and her warm sleep cardigan, she left her room in time to meet Alex as she came down the stairs.

"United front?" her sister asked.

"Sure."

Alex sent her a sideways look. "I kind of want to mess with him a little."

Payton's first instinct was protective. She almost objected. But then again, Alex wouldn't hurt him. Much. "Be my guest."

The two of them were already waiting on the porch, huddled close together against the bite of the wind, when Easton, in a hooded jacket, shoulders hunched against the rain, ran up the walk carrying the suitcase Payton had left at his house. He hesitated at the sight of them, but then kept on coming.

As soon as he ducked under the shelter of the porch roof, Alex folded her arms across her chest and took charge. "I'm Alex, Payton's other sister."

Easton set down the suitcase and pushed back the wet hood of his jacket. "It's good to finally meet you." He really did look exhausted. Payton's heart throbbed with sympathy in the cage of her chest. "I just wish it were under better circumstances."

Alex couldn't resist a jab. "I'm thinking restraining order. What about you?"

He shrugged. "I'm thinking apologizing—groveling, even."

"Just for the record here. You mean *you're* groveling?"

"Absolutely. Picture me on my knees. This mess is all my fault and I'm begging for forgiveness." He turned to Payton then, his eyes full of regret. "I screwed up. I should have told my parents everything before taking you to meet them. It was my job to deal with their ridiculous, unacceptable blowback by myself. I swear, I just didn't expect that reaction. They *want* both West and me to find the right woman, settle down, have kids. Never in a million years would I have guessed they would equate what happened to poor West six years ago to us and the boys."

Alex gave Payton a gentle poke with her elbow and spoke out of the corner of her mouth. "It's not much fun torturing him when he already feels so bad." She tipped her head toward the front door. "I'm just going to…"

Payton nodded. "Night, Alex." Her sister slipped back into the house.

Out near the henhouse, one of the roosters crowed. Even under the shelter of the porch roof, it was cold, windy and wet. Payton wrapped her sweater closer around her and considered inviting him in.

But no. Once she let him inside, she would only weaken further. Who could say what she might do—fall into his arms, let him convince her that everything would turn out fine if only she would let it go, forget the way his parents had just treated her?

Uh-uh. Better if they just talked out here.

Easton said, "Look. I get it. I do. I don't know how else to tell you how sorry I am. There is no reason you had to be subjected to any of that."

The rain drummed on the porch roof. A gust of wind tore at her hair. Payton wrapped her sweater more tightly around her. "You're right. You should have handled it differently, but I've been lying in my bed awake for a couple of hours now thinking it over and you know, I kind of get where your mom is coming from."

"You what?" He scowled. "Don't go making excuses for her. She is completely in the wrong with this."

"Easton, I would be suspicious, too, if when the boys are older, one of them suddenly shows up with a woman I know nothing about who claims to have had his child. I mean, the more I think it over, the more I see that Joyce was just being protective of her son."

"Suspicion is one thing. She could have asked to speak with me privately at some later point to voice her concerns. And by a later point, I mean not while you were still a guest in her house. I'm angry with her and I made sure she knows it. And no matter what her 'suspicions,' I'm a grown man, a responsible, mature man, one who doesn't need his mother to make his choices for him."

She gave a sad little laugh. "Well, yeah. You're right about that."

"Gee, thanks," he grumbled.

"And though I sympathize with your mother's need to protect her family, the way she came at me was pretty horrible. It's going to take me a while to get past that."

"Payton…" He started to reach for her.

She longed to fall into his arms. But she made herself step back. "No. Listen."

He let his arm drop to his side. "Say it."

"Things have to change, Easton. They really do."

"What do you mean?"

"I mean that yes, you and I have a lot to work out in terms of the boys, but all the marriage talk? It has to stop."

"What? No."

"Yeah. Beyond the fact that I would never marry

a man whose parents think I'm trying to entrap him, what happened last night was a wake-up call."

"Not true. What happened last night was my mother acting badly. And I swear, it's going to be okay. My mother will get over it."

Payton held her ground. "That's not the point."

"Then what is the point? In what way was last night a wake-up call?"

She really did want him to get it, to understand. "Look. I have enough insecurities, okay? To put it right out there, my mother was a self-absorbed flake with substance abuse issues. She was rarely around, and I still have no idea who my father might have been. I was the kid nobody wanted. That's bad enough. I'm not going to be the troublemaking gold digger in your family. I'm just not."

"That's not fair."

"Maybe not. But it's how I feel. And we *have* been moving too fast, anyway. We need to put the brakes on this budding romance we've got going on."

"Payton, no. You're just afraid. It's going to be all—"

"Stop!" She didn't realize she'd practically shouted the word until he winced. "Sorry. But we need to slow it down. Yes, the attraction is still there between us. Yes, we made two beautiful little boys together. But we are in no way ready to marry each other. You're here till after Christmas and you need to spend time getting to know your sons and thinking about how it's going to work out, about what you want in terms of time with the boys going forward and how to make that happen."

He looked down at his shoes and rubbed the back of his neck. "Slow it down, huh?"

Her throat felt tight. Did she really *want* to push him away? No. But she needed to. "We need to get our priorities straight. Our sons. They matter. We need to put our focus on them."

"And when are you going to be okay with me telling them I'm their dad?"

*I have no idea.* "It's too soon."

"When? Come on, Payton. Don't string me along."

He did have a point. She suggested, "How about we give it a month of you spending time with them, becoming a real part of their lives?"

He looked at her through watchful eyes, his strong jaw set. "So then, before Christmas. A month from today is December 20. We're telling them then. There will be no going back on that."

She made herself nod. "Yes. All right."

"Thanksgiving is next week. I expect to be invited to whatever goes on for Thanksgiving here at the farm." As if to punctuate his demand, one of the goats in the pasture next to the pear orchard let out a ridiculous honking sound. From the next pasture over, a horse neighed in response. Near the portable henhouse, that insomniac rooster crowed again.

Payton almost laughed. "*Whatever goes on?* We have turkey and a thousand sides, and we eat way too much."

"And I'm invited."

She longed to ask how his mother would take that, but somehow restrained herself. "Of course. We would love to have you join us over at Aunt Marilyn's for Thanksgiving dinner."

"Thank you, I'll be here. Tonight, I'll stop by to see the boys. And in the next few days, I want to take them out for pizza or burgers or whatever, just them and me."

Was it too soon for him to take them somewhere without her? Or did she just want it to be because she was scared of so many things? She didn't need her heart broken and every time he showed up for the boys, she would have to see him and be tempted and wish it could all work out for them, like in some fairy tale or a wonderful, happily-ever-after romance novel.

"Payton?"

She shivered a little. "Yes. I heard you. And okay, burgers or whatever whenever you can make the time, just you and the boys, is fine."

"And one more thing…"

"What?"

"You and me."

"Easton, I just said we can't—"

"I know what you said. But I still want a chance with you." His mouth curved in a half smile as his eyes turned tender, causing all manner of little furry creatures to dance around in her belly. "You need to stop being so terrified of relationships."

"Oh, do I?"

"Absolutely. And I have a plan to help you with that."

She let out a silly sound, something midway between a laugh and a snort. "Of course you do."

"I agree to your terms—but on the condition that for the next month, you will go out with me at least once a week."

"Go out where?"

"Doesn't matter. Dinner. A long walk in that orchard on the far side of the red barn, skiing at Mount Hood Meadows. We'll figure it out. I'll arrange for a sitter each time, so you don't have to ask your aunt or Josie to keep an eye on the boys."

"What does that mean, *at least* once a week?"

He chuckled. "You should see your face."

She glared up at him. "Do not make fun of me."

"I'm not. And yes, you have to go out with me at least once every week—and we won't hide it from the boys that we're dating."

"They're four, Easton. They don't know dating."

He only stared at her patiently. "Agreed?"

They faced off in the yellow glow of the porch light. The rain beat on the roof overhead and she kept her arms wrapped protectively around herself.

She felt scared. Terrified, really—of how much she wanted him, of getting her hopes up and being abandoned again as she was by the father she never knew, by her flighty mother. *And* by Easton himself five years ago—even if that was at least as much her fault as his.

"Well?" he asked softly.

She stared at him in his hooded gray jacket and dark jeans, his hair all tousled and his smile tempting enough to weaken her knees. Taking chances was scary. But it mattered so much, to think that he still wanted to—still wanted *her*, in spite of what had happened with his parents.

"Okay," she said, her voice breathy, a little ragged. "One date a week—at least."

His white teeth flashed as he smiled. "Well, all right. We have a deal."

Determined to convince Payton how much he wanted his sons *and* their mother, he showed up for his first visit with the boys at six that night.

Payton, wearing torn jeans and a frayed waffle-weave Henley, her hair piled up in a messy bun with a pencil stuck in the middle of it and her face scrubbed clean of any trace of makeup, answered the door. "We were just sitting down to eat."

"God, you are gorgeous. What are we having?"

She rolled her eyes so hard she was lucky she didn't fall over backward. "Chicken nuggets, homemade applesauce and steamed broccoli."

"My favorite."

With a snort-laugh, she let him in. "Hey, guys. Easton's here to see you…"

The boys sang out, "Hi, Easton!" in unison.

He washed his hands. Payton set him a place and offered a beer.

"Thank you, yes." He joined them at the table, where the boys explained he had to eat his broccoli, or he wouldn't get dessert.

"It's cupcakes!" announced Bailey with enthusiasm. "Auntie M made them."

Easton cleaned his plate, ate his cupcake and went upstairs to hang out with his sons until bedtime. Once the boys were tucked into bed, Payton tried to hustle him out the door.

"Not so fast." He pulled out a chair at the table.

"Make yourself at home," she grumbled. But at least she sat down, too. "What?"

"So I'm thinking date night tomorrow. Monday, I'll take the boys for burgers."

"You said you'd find a sitter for these dates

you're planning." Her bun kind of bobbed on her head as she spoke. It was the cutest thing.

He wished he could kiss her, but he had a hunch that wouldn't fly. Yet. "And I did find a sitter."

She slanted him a look of pure suspicion. "Did you get references?"

"You know her. Hazel Halstead?" The girl was thirteen and lived with her dad and older sister on the farm next door to Wild Rose.

"How did you know to call Hazel?"

"I called the number here at the farm and got your aunt. She said that Miles Halstead, a widower who owns the farm next door, has two teenage daughters and that the younger one sits for the boys all the time. Marilyn gave me the number and Hazel said she would be happy to babysit tomorrow night, so we're all set. She'll be here at seven and so will I." He couldn't resist teasing, "Objections?"

She reached up, yanked the pencil from her bun and stabbed it back in. "Seven is fine."

"Terrific."

And then she was up and ushering him out the door. He went reluctantly. Tomorrow, after all, was another day and they had a date for tomorrow night.

Sunday night, he took her to dinner at a nice little place in Hood River and then to a show. It went well, he thought. She let him hold her hand in the theater. He even got a quick peck of a kiss when he walked her to her door.

But she didn't invite him in.

He managed to get away at two the next day for burgers with the boys. After he'd hooked their booster seats in the back of his BMW, they climbed in and buckled up. Off they went to McDonald's.

Once they'd finished their Happy Meals, he planned to let them loose in the PlayPlace.

But there was a glitch. No PlayPlace.

The guy behind the counter—Ted, according to his nametag—said kids hardly used them anymore. They had tablets and phones to keep them busy now.

"Well, that's just wrong," Easton griped. Back when he and Weston were little, they'd loved the PlayPlace. He'd looked forward to seeing the boys jumping in the ball pit and climbing around in the tube maze.

"Sorry," said Ted. "Wish I could help you, man." He looked kind of glum, as though he too regretted the demise of the McDonald's playground.

Bailey tugged on Easton's sleeve. "Are you sad, Easton?"

Easton looked down at the honest concern on his son's upturned face and his heart went to mush. Gently, he patted Bailey's shoulder.

"Thanks for asking, Bailey. But don't worry. I'm okay."

"Try Heartwood Park," Ted suggested.

"Yeah!" Penn concurred.

Bailey agreed, too. "They have swings and a slide and everything there."

Ted gave them directions and off they went to swing on the swings, climb the play structure and slide down the slide.

Tuesday, it was rainy and cold. Easton visited the boys at home again.

Payton served mac and cheese with ham. After dinner, he and the twins went upstairs and played a learn-to-read game on one of their clunky blue plastic tablets. It was fun.

Or it was until Bailey accused his brother of not sharing.

"I do share!" Penn cried—and threw the tablet at Bailey.

Bailey wailed, "That hurt!"

Penn stuck out his chin. "Don't care!"

Easton tried desperately to figure out what had gone wrong and, more importantly, what he should do next. Luckily, Payton appeared at the top of the stairs just as Bailey informed Penn that he couldn't come to Bailey's birthday party.

Penn cried, "It's my birthday, too!" and burst into tears.

"Time-in, boys," called Payton. When they both

started to argue at once, Payton said, "Nope. Time-in. Sit quietly together for three minutes." She had her phone in her hand. "Then we will talk."

Red-faced, they each took a chair at the kid-size play table, where they mirrored each other exactly. Folding their arms across their little chests, they glared at each other.

Bailey muttered, "It's not fair. You started it."

"Did not."

"Did, too."

Payton said pleasantly, "Okay, we'll start that three minutes again."

After that, other than the occasional impatient sigh or injured moan, both boys kept their mouths shut. When three consecutive minutes had passed without any words from either boy, Payton had them all sit in a circle. "You, too, Easton."

He felt kind of sheepish as he joined the other three cross-legged in the middle of the play area floor. Really, he and Weston used to get into it now and then, too, way back in the day. Somehow, the conflicts had always worked themselves out. He consoled himself with that as Payton encouraged the boys to take turns talking about their feelings, and then began exploring ways they could work out their differences without fighting.

Later, when he and Payton came back downstairs after tooth brushing, story time and tucking in, she said, "Got a few minutes before you go?"

*For you, I've got a lifetime.* "Sure."

"Let's go in my office. As far as I know, the boys aren't big on eavesdropping—but just in case, my room has a door to shut."

He followed her into the large room on the other side of the stairs. Her bedroom took up the back half. The front was her office. She had her desk at the front window and a love seat under the window on the side wall.

"Let's sit down," she said. He took the love seat and she claimed the club chair opposite him.

Tonight, she wore a giant green PSU Vikings sweatshirt, yoga pants and heavy socks printed with penguins. As she drew her legs up and crossed them on the chair cushion, he wished he could scoop her up, plop her down on his lap and steal at least one kiss.

"I just wanted to be sure you weren't traumatized by the temper tantrums," she said.

"I'm okay. I may be only a beginner as a dad, but I was a kid once. West and I used to get pretty rowdy. Back then, though, we had time-*outs*."

"Yeah, time-outs can be a bit isolating, so we have time-ins."

"Ah. Makes sense." He confessed, "I did freak out there for a minute. I had no idea what to do when Penn threw his tablet. Yesterday at McDonald's popped into my mind. They were a couple of angels that day. But how would I have managed if they'd gone after each other right there at the table over their Happy Meals?"

She laughed. "The good news is that their public displays are rare now. But when they do happen, I just try to herd them as gently as possible to the car. Then we can have a time-in together and get into coping strategies, the way we did tonight."

"By 'coping strategies,' you mean getting them talking about what they felt when they got angry and how to work things out without fighting?"

"Exactly—and really, you're doing great. You're a natural in the dad department. They love you already."

Did he feel like the ruler of the universe at that moment? Yep. "I, um, appreciate that."

"It's the truth."

"And I have a question."

"Go for it."

"When they started arguing about their birthday party, I realized I didn't know when their birthday was—but that it couldn't be coming up anytime soon, right?"

"It's July 25."

"And they're already fighting about the party and who's not invited?"

"Easton. When you're four, birthday parties are serious business."

"Right. I get that." If he did kiss her now, would

they end up in her bed? Was it wrong to be thinking about peeling off those yoga pants during a discussion of how to parent more effectively?

Well, he didn't care if it was wrong. He wanted to kiss her, and he longed to end up in her bed.

But that didn't happen—not that night, anyway. A moment later, she was ushering him to the door.

Every day that passed, Payton had a harder time remembering that she and Easton needed to agree on a plan for their lives as coparents—and no more.

She clung to all the reasons they would never make it as a couple. His work mattered to him and kept him in Seattle. Her aunt and her sister needed her. She couldn't see herself living anywhere else but Wild Rose Farm. She and Easton really hadn't known each other that long—because five years of not knowing where the hell the other one was or how to reach out and make contact did not count as "knowing each other."

They'd had one long-ago week together and the six weeks since he'd appeared at her booth on the last market day of the season. Seven weeks total—*that* was how long they'd known each other.

Oh, and his mother thought she was a gold-digging skank—his father, too, she had to assume, though Myron hadn't been nearly as vocal about it as Joyce. The cruel things Joyce had said that night in Seattle rankled every time she thought of them.

And yet, when Easton showed up at noon on Thanksgiving Day, and she stood on the porch of her aunt's cottage as the kids ran out to greet him, all she could think of was how *right* it would be—the four of them together, a real family. The boys jumped around him in circles, thrilled at the sight of him. And despite the numerous valid reasons she had to keep Easton at a distance, that feeling of rightness?

It wouldn't go away. It dogged her all that day. He'd brought a gorgeous cranberry streusel pie from the best bakery in town and two nice bottles of white wine to contribute to the feast. He helped the boys finish up their centerpiece of fall leaves and construction-paper turkeys, and then supervised them as they set the Thanksgiving table. He volunteered to carve the turkey.

But Ernesto Bezzini got that job.

Ernesto's visit with his old friend Tom Huckston had been extended indefinitely, or so it appeared. Supposedly, Ernesto remained a guest of the Huckstons. But lately, he spent most of his time at Aunt Marilyn's.

As for Auntie M, she looked a decade younger, and she never stopped smiling.

When they all sat down to eat, Auntie M had

them hold hands around the table the way she did every Thanksgiving. They took turns, each of them naming at least one thing they were thankful for. The boys had about ten things each—things like macaroni and cheese, chocolate pie, ladybugs and Tink, who waited under the table for someone to sneak her a bit of turkey now and then. Bailey and Penn were also grateful for everyone at the table and they named them off one by one.

Easton's turn came next. "I'm grateful to be here," he said. "Grateful for all of you. Especially Penn and Bailey and Payton."

Payton shouldn't have glanced up, but she did. He gave her one of those smiles that made her wonder what was wrong with her to ever say no to him. Penn and Bailey giggled and elbowed each other.

"Enough, you two," Payton said in a whisper. The boys fell silent, and the gratefulness continued around the table. When Payton's turn came, she named everyone at the table, too.

Alex, who'd arrived the night before and would probably be heading back to Portland sometime after dinner, nudged Payton with her elbow. When Payton slid her a glance, Alex made a kissy face at her and cast a significant glance at Easton.

Payton took the high road and serenely bowed her head again.

The rest of the day went beautifully, Payton

thought. Alex left at a little after eight, promising as she did every year to stay longer when she came for Christmas. Payton would believe that when she saw it.

At eight thirty, Payton and Easton took the boys back to her cottage. Easton took charge, hustling the yawning kids upstairs and tucking them into their beds.

When he came down a half hour later, she met him at the base of the stairs. "They give you any grief?"

"Nope. They're beat. I think they're probably asleep already." He stood on the last step, the light above her little square of entryway picking out strands of bronze and gold in his hair. His eyes were oceans she kind of wished she might drown in. He said softly, "It was a good day."

"Yeah. So good. I was surprised when you said you wanted to come here to the farm for Thanksgiving."

"Where else would I want to be?"

"Well, your mom strikes me as someone who would expect her family at her house for all the big holiday celebrations."

"She is. But times change. Priorities do, too." He came down that last step. She backed up to make room.

And he lifted a hand—slowly, giving her every chance to back away again.

She didn't. She *couldn't*. Her body, her heart, her whole being felt magnetized.

To him.

Sparks cascaded through her as his fingers brushed her cheek. He tipped up her chin.

She sighed in delight as his lips covered hers.

When he lifted his head, she said, "Stay." Taking his hand, she led him into her room, where she closed the door quietly and engaged the privacy lock.

Payton woke before dawn to find Easton sound asleep beside her.

He caught her hand when she tried to slip from the bed. "No, you don't." He pulled her in close again and she snuggled against his warm, bare chest. "You have to work today?"

"Nope."

His lips brushed the crown of her head. "You do Black Friday?"

"Naw. I have hungry goats, chickens and a number of other critters to feed right now. Later, we have breakfast at my aunt's cottage. Join us?"

"Yes."

She tried to pull away and he held on. Laughing, she pushed at his chest. "Gotta go."

Reluctantly, he released her.

She switched on the lamp and pulled on old jeans, a sweatshirt and heavy socks. "Help yourself to coffee or whatever. Since you're here, I won't drag Josie over to snooze on the sofa and keep an eye out for the boys."

"Works for me." He was up on an elbow, all rumpled and sexy looking.

"If the boys come down give them fruit but remind them there will be breakfast at Auntie M's."

"Will do."

She moved close again for one last kiss—and managed to resist the temptation to crawl back into the warm cocoon of covers with him.

Pausing at the bedroom door, she promised, "I won't be that long..."

When she game back inside an hour later, she found Easton and the boys eating sliced apples and pears at the kitchen table, the boys in their pj's, Easton in the same clothes he'd worn yesterday.

The boys threw on their jackets over their pajamas and they all trooped across the way to Marilyn's, where her aunt and Ernesto served everyone breakfast.

Easton spent the day right there at the farm.

That night after the boys were tucked into bed, he took her in his arms, kissed her slow and deep and whispered, "I want to stay."

When exactly had she forgotten that she should be saying no to him? "Nothing is settled," she warned.

"I get it."

"The boys…"

"What? Say it."

"I know they're only four, but I don't want to confuse them. I can't have them thinking you live here. You don't live here, Easton."

"Let me stay." He kissed her again. "Just for a few hours. Not overnight…"

He was too close, too tempting. Too…everything.

She did what both her heart and her body wanted. She led him to her bed.

He was gone before midnight. She'd no sooner ushered him out the door than she wished she'd begged him to stay. Her spirits lifted when he called the next morning to remind her it was date night.

Hazel Halstead arrived at six that evening and Payton and Easton went to Barone's for dinner. Afterward, he took her to his house on the river. She stayed later than she should have.

Sunday, he showed up at lunchtime. She didn't know who was happier to see him—her, or the boys. They spent the day together, like the family she'd again started to hope they might someday be.

Monday brought a return to business as usual. Easton had to work all day. Payton took the boys to preschool. Marilyn would pick them up at noon.

Back at home in her office, she consulted with her editor on a title change for *Queen of Jade and Sorrow* and then got down to working on the manuscript. She'd written eight usable pages and had really hit her stride when a truck and double horse trailer pulled up out in front.

Payton stared with her mouth hanging open as Easton's dad, in jeans, cowboy boots, a shearling jacket and a Seahawks cap got out on the passenger side and came up the walk.

## Chapter Ten

Payton pulled open the door before Myron could knock. She demanded, "Did Easton give you my address?"

"Hey! It's okay." Easton's dad put up both hands. "I come in peace."

"I asked you a simple question."

Myron swept off his cap. "My son isn't speaking to me, so no. He gave me no information about how to get here. I found the address on the Wild Rose Farm website and your house was the first along the driveway. If you hadn't answered the door, I'd have tried the other two."

Another man dressed much like Myron, but with a big cowboy hat instead of a Seahawks cap, emerged from behind the wheel of the truck and headed for the end of the horse trailer. When he got there, he put down a ramp and opened the doors.

"Who is that guy? What's going on, Myron?"

"That's my friend, Paco Ravelle. We grew up together."

"Of course you did."

Myron seemed to take zero offense at her sarcastic tone. "Paco owns a gorgeous horse property near Carnation, a half hour from Seattle. Raises Arabians and POAs."

"P-O huh?" She watched the man named Paco as he unlocked the horse trailer.

"Pony of the Americas," Myron provided in a hopeful tone. "It's a breed. An Arabian/Appaloosa/Shetland pony cross. I grew up on a ranch near Carnation, learned to ride young. My boys were raised in Seattle, true. But I saw to it that both of them knew how to appreciate and care for a horse."

As she stared in disbelief, Paco led a beautiful, brown-spotted white pony from the trailer. He hitched the pony's lead to the back of the trailer and went up the ramp again, descending a moment later with another pony that looked very much like the first one, but with more brown in its coat.

Myron, who'd turned to follow her gaze, faced her again with a giant grin. "I'm contrite, Payton. I want to meet my grandsons—and I've never been a man who's squeamish about certain kinds of bribery."

"You've got to be kidding me." She skewered him with her coldest stare.

Myron just kept on talking. "It's like this. I get

it, Payton. I do. Joyce is all wrong about you. I'm so sorry. She's always been hotheaded—though to her credit, in the past decade or so, she's learned to slow down her response, go easier, look before the big leap, if you get my drift..." He waited for a reply.

She gave him a reluctant "Whatever you say."

"And I, well, I love my wife. She and our boys are my whole life. I can get kind of swept right along with her when she turns all fiery and fierce. I might be an old man, but frankly, when she gets like that, it's hot—and yeah, that's my excuse for my behavior a week and a half ago. But after Easton read us the riot act and stormed out, and then Weston called us a pair of damn fools, well, I started to feel a tad ashamed. Within a couple of days, I tried getting Joyce to see that we were in the wrong."

"And how'd that go for you?" Payton folded her arms across her middle.

"I've gotten nowhere with her," he admitted. "Yet." He made a sad face. "My wife is the only one for me. Unfortunately, the woman has no shortage of stubbornness and pride. She needs to work her way through that before she'll be ready to admit she screwed up."

"Are you trying to reassure me somehow? Because it's not working."

"I'll try harder. Payton, it's now obvious to me

that Easton loves you. You're a fine woman trying to do the right thing—and I see clearly now that the situation between the two of you is nothing like what happened with Weston six years ago."

"Thank you. As for your wife, did it ever occur to you that maybe she'll never see the light about me?"

He fiddled nervously with the bill of his hat. "Trust me, she will come around eventually. And when she does, I promise you, she'll be as protective of you as she is of our boys."

Was she reassured? Not really. Not about Joyce. But already, she'd pretty much forgiven Myron. He clearly *was* trying. And trying mattered. "Ponies, Myron? It's a lot."

"And aren't they the cutest two ponies you ever saw?" Down at the trailer, Paco swept off his hat and bowed. Myron went on, "One for each of my grandsons—and I know that caring for a horse can get expensive. I'm prepared to send a monthly check for their upkeep. And you don't have to say it. I get it. I'm shameless. I want my grandsons to love me and I'm not above buying their affection—and yours if you're the least susceptible." He gave her a wink. "You just need to tell me what you want. Chances are I can make it happen."

She couldn't help laughing. "Sorry, but uh-uh.

Contrary to your wife's mistaken opinion, I can't be bought. The kids, maybe. But not me."

"Where are they?" His eyes gleamed with excitement. "I can't wait to meet them."

So much for a twenty-page day on the book shortly to be titled something other than *Queen of Jade and Sorrow.* "Yeah, well. We need to talk about that. Why don't you and Paco come on in and have some coffee."

"I was afraid you'd never ask." Myron's sun-lined, handsome face broke into that blinding smile again, a smile that reminded her way too sharply of the man who'd fathered her children.

Inside, she'd barely brewed Myron and Paco each a cup before Auntie M and Ernesto appeared.

"We saw you had company and noticed the two lovely ponies waiting out in front," said Marilyn with that smile that said it all—including *I'm here and I've got your back, baby.* "Thought we should make sure everything's all right."

"It's fine." Payton kissed her aunt's soft cheek. "Coffee?"

"We would love some."

So they all five gathered around the kitchen table. Payton made introductions and then told Myron the rules. "This is a farm, so yes. You can leave the ponies here and *eventually* you can give them to Penn and Bailey."

"How long will it be until 'eventually'?"

"A while. They don't know yet that Easton is their father."

"But why not?"

It was a very good question. She tried to answer thoughtfully. "Easton and I haven't agreed on where we're going yet—as a couple."

Myron kind of hung his head. "Because of what happened a week and a half ago?"

She looked around the table at all the serious faces. "Well, I guess to be honest, I would have to say that factored in. But, Myron, don't look so sad. Easton and I only knew each other for a week five years ago. We have stuff to figure out. And the boys are so young. If they were older and had a better understanding of what they've been missing, I would have agreed to tell them immediately. But I asked Easton to wait a little, to let them get to know him first and also to give Easton and me time to possibly make decisions about the future."

"I understand. I guess…"

She resisted the urge to pat his arm reassuringly. "On the brighter side, yes, they do need to know, and soon. We've agreed on a date. By the twentieth of December, we will tell them the truth no matter what. Once that happens, it's between you and Easton when you introduce yourself as their grandfather."

"I don't like it, though I suppose I understand."

He held her gaze. "But I want to meet them today—as Easton's dad?"

"Of course, as long as Easton's on board. You need to talk to him about it first."

Myron slanted her a look. "I did mention he's not speaking to me?"

"You did, yes. We should fix that." She got out her phone.

"You'll call him? For me?"

"For both of you, yes."

"You're a fine gal, Payton." Myron looked a bit misty-eyed. Really, so did the rest of them—and Payton couldn't hide a small sniffle of her own.

"Thank you." She called Easton, who didn't answer at first, but then called her right back. When she explained the situation, he called his father.

Myron went out on the porch to speak with him privately. When he came in, he was smiling. "All right. I have permission to meet my grandsons tonight, after Easton is finished at the project. He will introduce me—as long as that's all right with you, Payton?"

"Perfect."

"I'm so glad. And Paco and I will get out of your hair for now."

Auntie M rose and offered to show them where to pasture the ponies. Payton gave her a hug in thanks.

A few minutes later, she was able to lock herself in her office again and make those twenty pages happen, after all.

That night, Easton and Myron showed up with enough takeout for everyone at the farm, including a red velvet cake for dessert. The boys got to meet "Easton's dad." Paco, Payton learned, had headed home. Myron would fly back in the next few days.

After the takeout feast, the boys took Easton and Myron upstairs to build a Duplo space station and play board games. It went well, Payton thought. When Easton and his dad left for the night, the boys hugged them both and urged them to come back and play anytime.

"And it's okay if you bring another cake, too," suggested Penn.

Myron had tears in his eyes as they went out the door.

Tuesday, he showed up at a little after one in the afternoon and took the boys out to meet the ponies. He'd bought them all the equipment they would need to ride, and he set out to teach them the basics of caring for a horse.

Myron was good with the kids and generally helpful. Payton had zero objection when he came by both Wednesday and Thursday to lavish attention on her sons.

Friday, Payton took the day off and let Penn and Bailey stay home from day care. Easton and his dad arrived at 9:00 a.m. Bundled up warmly, they all spent some time at the pasture with the ponies. Myron encouraged the boys to come up with names. They settled on Deke and Dotty.

A little later, they all piled into the Toyota Tundra Payton had bought when her ancient Tacoma finally gave up the ghost. She took them to a nearby tree farm. Together, they cut down a tree and brought it home to the cottage. Payton put on the Christmas tunes and everyone helped bring the decorations up from the basement. Father, son and grandsons all pitched in to decorate.

Once the tree, crowned with an angel, stood in the front window dressed in tinsel, shiny balls and hundreds of tiny lights, Payton turned off the Christmas favorites and got out the seventy-year-old Gibson guitar that Auntie M had given her when she was thirteen. Auntie M had inherited the guitar from Grandma Dahl, who'd died before Payton was born.

For over an hour, Payton played Christmas classics and they all sang along. Even the boys stuck with it, sitting cross-legged, side by side, swaying their upper bodies to the music, singing along on every song. Already, they knew most of them by heart.

"You boys sure know a lot of Christmas songs," Myron said with admiration.

"We sing them every Christmas!" Penn explained proudly.

"Yeah," Bailey added, "Ever since we were *very* small."

Before he and Easton left that night, Myron asked to talk to Payton for a moment, just the two of them. Easton took the boys upstairs to get ready for bed while his dad and Payton put on jackets and went out into the almost-winter night.

As they strolled the graveled driveway that circled between the cottages, Myron said, "I'm on my way home in the morning."

She stopped and faced him. "It's been good to get to know you a little. To introduce you to the boys."

"It's been amazing," he replied in a tone close to reverence.

They walked on.

He said, "I've been wondering…"

"Yes?"

"Penn and Bailey are interesting names…"

She slanted him a wry glance. "What are you getting at, Myron?"

"Are the boys named for people you know?"

"Nope. I wanted them to have names all their own. I liked the sound of Penn and of Bailey. The names go together well—and yet they're not alike. They're individual. I knew that people would always see the similarities between them, but they're also two distinct people and I wanted their names to be a reminder of that."

"Not like say, Easton and Weston."

She laughed outright. "Your words, not mine. Honestly, though, I happen to like Easton and Weston."

"Joyce chose them. She has a whimsical side." He seemed wistful.

"You miss her."

He gave a slow nod. "I do. Sadly, it's one of those periods in our marriage when we're not communicating, if you know what I mean."

"I'm sorry to be the cause of that."

"You're not. In time, Joyce will see that—and please don't worry about Joyce and me, Payton. My wife and I have been together for a long time. Sometimes, the going gets rough, but we always make it through. This time will be no different."

By then, they'd circled the driveway. They kept walking past Payton's cottage and stopped midway between her place and Josie's.

Hunching down into the collar of his jacket, his breath coming out as fog, Myron announced, "I want to come back at Christmastime."

"You mean after the boys know that Easton's their dad."

He nodded. "When I come back, I want to tell

them I'm their grandfather and formally give them their ponies."

Myron and the boys had spent a lot of time the past few days with Dotty and Deke. The twins brought the ponies treats of apples and carrots, learned the rudiments of grooming and had even tried out the pony saddles Myron had bought.

Payton had learned to ride young, as had both her sisters. Some of her fondest memories were of riding the mules and horses Auntie M kept on the farm. Payton's sons would do the same, partly thanks to their grandfather. She loved that Myron had taken that kind of care with them, that he not only showed up with extravagant gifts, but he also took the time and had the patience to teach Penn and Bailey how to care for those gifts.

Myron said, "I also want to spend time with them on a regular basis."

"I'm glad—and you're welcome here, whenever you can come. You're great with them and they already love you."

A smile lit up his face. "I really do hope you end up saying yes to my son."

"Oh, Myron." She almost hugged him then. "We will definitely keep you posted on that."

"Thank you. And about Joyce…?"

She wrapped her coat more tightly around her. "What?"

"She *will* come around. When she does, I hope you'll be willing to forgive her."

Payton didn't know how to answer him. An actual relationship between her and Joyce seemed something that they needed to create themselves. And if Joyce wanted to make amends, wouldn't she be here now? "I hope she does come around. If and when she does, I promise to keep an open mind with her."

Myron made a low, thoughtful sound. "Guess I can't ask for more." Then he held out his arms. "Got a goodbye hug for your future father-in-law?"

"Myron," she chided. "Don't push your luck."

He lifted a shoulder in a half shrug. "I like to think positive."

"And I admire your upbeat attitude." Stepping forward, she let him enfold her.

"All right, then," he said as he released her. "Let's go in so I can say goodbye to my two favorite boys."

The next morning, Saturday, Easton showed up at breakfast time. Payton fried extra bacon and eggs. He sat down to eat with her, Josie and the twins.

After breakfast, they all went out to the east pasture to pay a visit to Dotty and Deke. The grown-ups helped the boys tack up so they could enjoy a short, slow ride between the east and west pastures.

That night was date night. Easton took her to dinner and then to his place. He brought her home at a little after eleven. They stood kissing on the porch for another ten minutes before she finally went inside.

In the first full week of December, Easton appeared at the farm every evening after he finished work at the inn. Sometimes he brought takeout. Sometimes Payton cooked. After the meal, he would hang out with the boys until their bedtime.

The three of them had secret projects upstairs, projects that required wrapping paper and holiday ribbon. Such a shocker when they'd march proudly down the stairs to put freshly wrapped gifts under the tree. Most of their wrapping efforts involved a lot of wrinkled Christmas paper and way too much tape. Somehow, to Payton, that only made the gifts all the more beautiful.

Her secret truth? She found watching him and the boys together downright ovulation-inducing. Like his dad, Easton was great with them. Whatever mean thoughts she might have about Joyce, she believed Joyce must have been an excellent mom to Easton and Weston when they were growing up, just as Myron could only have been a terrific dad.

What would that be like, she wondered? To

grow up at the center of your mom and dad's life? To have the head start of knowing you were wanted, cherished by the two people who had brought you into the world? That they had a deep bond, your parents, that nothing could break them apart?

Whatever happened with her and Easton, she knew now that her sons wouldn't have to wonder what it might be like to have a dad. She felt certain now that they would not only have her, their aunts and great-aunt and a baby cousin in the next couple of months, but also a grandfather who loved them—and probably, in time, a grandma, too.

Thursday late in the afternoon, when Easton was still at the inn and the boys had gone out to help Auntie M with evening chores, Kyle dropped by with his girlfriend, Olga. Olga had a ring on her finger.

Shyly, happily, Kyle explained, "She said yes."

Payton let out a shout of pure glee and grabbed him in a hug, reaching out an arm to grab Olga tightly, too.

Last year in June, when she and Kyle had broken off their engagement, he'd confessed that all his life, he'd been waiting for Payton to see that he was the one for her.

*But I get it now*, he'd said sadly. *I've been hold-*

*ing on to the idea of you, but the real you just doesn't love me that way.*

And then she'd burst into tears and he'd hugged her and said it was okay. She hadn't believed him at the time. For a while after the breakup, she'd feared she'd destroyed their friendship.

But she hadn't. They really were still good friends. And every time she saw him with Olga, she felt pure joy that he'd finally found what he'd been looking for.

"What are you doing Saturday night?" she asked.

Olga and Kyle share a look. "Um, nothing special," Olga replied.

"Good. I'm throwing you an engagement party in the event barn. It's going to be fabulous."

Both Kyle and Olga said she shouldn't, *they* couldn't, it was way too much work, especially on such short notice.

Payton insisted, "It's happening. Stop saying no and start calling all your friends…"

By Saturday night, the guest list had swelled to everyone in the surrounding neighborhood of small farms. No one was left out. The kids came and so did the grandparents. Olga had a lot of friends in town, so they came, too.

It was rainy and cold outside—and cozy and warm inside with a couple of barn heaters going.

A lot of the guests had pitched in that day to

decorate the barn with party lights and Christmas trees. Several local musicians showed up, so they had live music and dancing. Payton brought her grandmother's Gibson and sat in for a while.

Just about everyone got out on the floor, including Auntie M and Ernesto—and Penn and Bailey, both of whom liked to dance in circles, with their hands in the air. Easton whipped out his phone and took a bunch of pictures of the boys getting their four-year-old groove on.

Josie, who tired more easily now at almost seven months along, took the boys home to bed at a little before nine. Most of the other children went home around that time, too.

A little later, Olga, who had a gorgeous alto voice, sang "Make You Feel My Love" to Kyle. By the time she finished that song, there wasn't a dry eye in the barn. Kyle, who'd always been a quiet, low-key sort of guy, grabbed his new fiancée and kissed her so hard and deep, somebody shouted, "Get a room!"

Payton thought of Easton—back during that first, too-brief week five years ago—explaining that growing up, he and Weston used to wish their mom and dad would get a room. About then, she spotted him, over by one of the refreshment tables chatting with Ernesto. Easton raised his beer to her, and she smiled through her sentimental tears.

They danced together late into the night as the

rain beat a steady rhythm on the roof of the barn. She was so happy for Kyle and Olga, so pleased that her sons would grow up with a father who loved and cared for them.

As she swayed in Easton's arms, everything seemed so possible. At that moment, she had no fear of giving her heart completely. She felt absolute trust in the man who held her, that he would never again disappear, never leave her behind.

Very late, after everyone had left, they turned off the lights and the heaters and ran through the rain to her house, where Josie lay dozing on the sofa.

Josie put on her shoes and her coat, gave Payton a hug and announced, "Auntie M said to tell you she and Ernesto will do the morning chores tomorrow. You can sleep in." The sisters snickered together. With two four-year-olds in the house, Payton would be lucky to sleep until dawn.

She walked Josie out to the porch, waiting until her sister went in her own front door. When she turned to go back inside, Easton was there, in the doorway, watching her, his eyes dark, full of heat and wanting.

"Come here." He caught her hand and reeled her in.

His lips touched hers and the cold, wet night turned to magic. The ozone smell of the rain was so sweet and Easton's warm arms surrounded her, protecting her, cherishing her.

"Stay," she whispered when he lifted his head.

He pulled her into the cottage and shut and locked the door.

She woke at dawn, her eyes drifting open to find Easton smiling at her from the other pillow.

"Any minute, Penn and Bailey will be pounding on the bedroom door," she warned. Last time he'd spent the night in her bed, Thanksgiving night, she'd left him to tackle morning chores before the boys came down. This time, the boys would find them in the bedroom together.

Why did that seem somehow more meaningful?

He freed a hand from the covers and his warm fingers ghosted over her cheek as he combed her sleep-tangled hair out of her eyes and guided the snarled strands behind her ear. His touch, light as a breath, caused a sweet havoc of sensation all through her—heat in her belly, shivers down her arms, longing racing along every nerve.

"Then what?" he asked, his voice lazy and low as he continued to stroke his fingers through her hair. "Should I hide under the bed?"

"No."

"You want me to climb out the window?"

"Very funny. What I'm saying is, we should

just let them in." Terror went zipping through her at what she'd just suggested. Yet she didn't want to take the words back. "It's time. I know it."

He took her mouth in a hard, quick kiss. "Time to...?"

"Tell them that you're their dad."

His eyes lit up. "You mean that." It wasn't a question.

She confirmed it, anyway. "I do." And right then, as if on cue, she heard giggles on the stairs.

"Here they come," he said.

"Put your pants on." Rolling away from him, she darted to the door. As she grabbed her flannel pj's off the hook and yanked them on, Easton donned his pants and sweater from last night.

"Mom!" A knock on the door. The young voice turned wheedling. "It's morning..."

"We're *hungry*!" an identical voice called.

She turned to the barefoot man with sleep-scrambled hair who stood by the bed. "Ready?"

His grin spread ear to ear. "Let 'em in."

She pulled open the door. "Morning..."

"Mom, we..." Penn's eyes lit up. "Easton! You're still here."

"Yes, I am."

Both boys darted around her to run to him. He scooped up Bailey, who reached him first, and gathered Penn close to his side. "Hi, guys. How you doin'?"

"We're hungry," said Penn.

"And we don't get to do sleepovers yet." Bailey put on his pouty face.

Penn added, "Mom says not till we're six at least." He took Easton's hand. "Come on. You can have breakfast with us. Mom, can we have pancakes?"

Easton was watching her now, waiting for a signal as to how to begin.

"I think pancakes can be arranged," she said. "And then Easton and I have something special to talk to you about."

A half an hour later, they'd demolished a high stack of pancakes and Easton was nothing short of a nervous wreck. He kept waiting for one of the boys to ask what his mom wanted to say to them. But both twins seemed to have completely forgotten the "something special" their mother had promised they would talk about after breakfast.

Not that it mattered. Whether one of the boys asked or not, the moment had finally come when he could tell his sons that he was their dad.

Unfortunately, he had no idea where to begin. There had to be a book about how to do this, didn't there? At least he should have looked it up online.

"Can we be et-scused?" asked Bailey.

"Carry your plates to the sink," said Payton, looking so calm and sure. She should bottle that and share it with him, Easton thought. "And then come back and sit down," she added. "We have some good news for you."

The boys obediently trotted over to the sink, put their plastic plates, cups and flatware on the counter—and then returned.

"What good news?" demanded Penn, as they clambered up into their booster seats again.

*I'm your father!* Easton wanted to shout. Somehow, he quelled that urge. It was obvious he would be better off taking his cues from the expert, Payton.

She drank a sip of her coffee. "Do you remember how a few months ago you guys asked me why you didn't have a dad like Damien and Krystal at day care?"

Both boys gave slow, solemn nods. Bailey said, "You said we had a dad, but you didn't know where he was."

"Yes. I said I couldn't find him but that I would keep looking and maybe someday you would get to meet him."

Penn's expression had darkened. He accused, "You lost our dad."

And all of a sudden, Payton didn't seem quite so self-assured. "Yes. I…I did. We lost each other. I didn't know how to get in touch with him and he didn't know where I was, either."

Dead silence. Both boys sat impossibly still, waiting for whatever she would say next.

And Easton couldn't stay silent a second longer. "I'm the one," he blurted out. "I'm your dad."

Payton sucked in a sharp breath as two pairs of stunned blue eyes swung his way.

"You're our daddy?" whispered Bailey, awestruck.

Easton's heart hung suspended inside his chest—and then resumed beating so hard and fast, he knew it would detonate. Was he having a heart attack? Maybe a stroke?

"I am your dad, yes," he finally made himself answer his son.

Bailey climbed off his seat and came straight to him. Easton got down onto one knee and opened his arms. Bailey, his hands a little sticky from pancake syrup, grabbed him around the neck. "You're here," he whispered fervently. "You found us."

"Yes. And I am so glad I did." Easton held out an arm for Penn, who'd remained in his plastic seat and regarded him warily. "Penn?"

Penn didn't budge. "Why didn't you tell us before?"

*Because Payton wanted to wait.* Had she been wrong? Should he have insisted they tell the boys right away?

One thing seemed for certain. Blaming their mother wouldn't be good for anyone. "I'm telling you now. And I did have a reason for holding back. I wanted you to get to know me a little, to be happy to find out that I'm your dad."

"I am happy." Bailey hugged him harder.

Penn still held back. "When are you going away again?"

There was only one answer to that question. "Never."

That seemed to work for Penn. He jumped down and joined the hug.

Best. Moment. Ever. He had one arm around each of his sons, all three of them holding on tight.

Yeah, for a minute or two there, he thought he'd blown this important conversation all to hell. Yet somehow, it had come out right.

Glancing up, he found Payton watching them, her eyes shiny with unshed tears. "Come here," he mouthed the words at her.

She gave him a wobbly, hopeful little smile. But she stayed in her chair.

## *Chapter Eleven*

Easton spent all of Sunday at the farm. It rained a lot, but when the sky cleared for a while in the afternoon, he and Payton and the boys went out to visit Deke and Dotty. The boys got to ride and practice grooming the ponies.

The afternoon turned colder. A light snow began to fall—not enough to stick. But still, it was beautiful drifting down. The lights of the tree they'd all decorated together glowed in the front window and the boys stood on the front walk, their faces turned up to the gray sky, catching snowflakes on their tongues.

Marilyn cooked dinner for everyone at her house.

Easton was flying high. This, after all, a cozy day with his sons and their mother, who happened to be the woman he loved, dinner with the family—it pretty much defined everything he wanted. He needed more days with Payton and the boys. They all needed to be together, to live together as a family.

Yeah, he knew he'd promised her not to push too fast.

But what was too fast, really? He wanted her for his wife. He wanted them all to be together. They could work out all the details as they went along.

Payton had doubts, though. He could see them, lurking, dark shadows in her eyes.

She waited until the boys were in bed to say quietly, "We need to talk." She didn't even try to put on a smile.

He followed her into her room, watched her shut the door and turn the privacy lock. "What happened? What's wrong?"

"Sit down." She said it too gently.

He took the club chair. "Talk to me, Payton."

She settled into the love seat. "Today, you told the boys you would never leave."

"Because I won't."

She pinched up her mouth at him, reminding him of Penn that morning, wary. Doubtful. "Easton. Kids are so literal."

And that meant exactly what? "Okay, I get that…"

She sat forward and back, as though she couldn't get comfortable. "We haven't settled anything— you know that. When you say you'll never leave, they take that to mean you'll always be here, where they are, in Heartwood. At Wild Rose Farm."

"Payton. Words like *never* and *always* are relative."

"Not to a four-year-old. Things are very simple when you're four. People are there. Or they're not."

"Look. What I meant by 'never' was that I would always be in their lives, that they can count on me, no matter what."

"Ah." She folded her hands in her lap, looked down at them—and caved. "Well. When you put it that way, yes. That works."

Now he felt strangely confused. Sometimes, she seemed so on top of every little thing. And other times, like now, he thought she had no more idea how to navigate parenthood than he did. "So then, do you want me to talk to them again, and, er, put it that way?"

"God no—I mean, we need *not* to overexplain. We'll only confuse them. We wait."

"Until…?"

"They ask more questions. And they will, in time. Probably when you leave, and they ask why you left when you said you never would."

"Did I say I was leaving?"

"Easton, you live in Seattle. You're not going to be here in Heartwood all the time. It's a fact." His gut twisted. What was she getting at? It didn't sound good. But then she said, "You're right, though."

Now he was thoroughly confused. "I am?"

"I mean, I only wanted to talk to you about how your saying that you'll never leave has to be dealt with going forward—that's all. They might be upset the first time you're gone for any serious stretch of time. But then they'll see that you always come back. Also, your dad is all in with them. From what Myron says, your mom will get on board at some point. You'll take them to Seattle. They will begin to understand that they can count on you, that you take care of them, that you're there for them. That if they don't see you for a while, you will always come back."

"Payton, even when I'm physically away from them for a while for one reason or another, Seattle isn't the other side of the moon. And they can always get in touch with me. We can FaceTime. Whatever."

"Well." She shifted, drew her legs up, put her feet down on the floor again. "You're right. I, um, well, maybe I'm making too much of this."

*You think?* "Payton…" He got up and sat down beside her on the love seat.

She frowned at him. "Yeah?"

He took her hand. She let him take it, but she continued to watch him as though he might be about to do something scary. "This conversation…"

"Hmm?"

"Is it really about the boys?"

* * *

Payton knew she'd messed up, made way too big a deal of a minor issue. "Of course it's about the boys." And it was.

Okay, maybe she did tend to see potential problems where there were none. She needed to watch that. Easton *was* dependable and he'd handled the big reveal of his fatherhood beautifully. Looking back, she could see that they should have discussed how they would navigate the conversation beforehand. But she'd just dumped him right into the deep end—and he'd started swimming. He'd managed beautifully.

He watched her through eyes that saw way too much. "I'll ask you again. Are you sure this is about the boys?"

Defensiveness tightened the muscles at the back of her neck. "What are you getting at? Just say it."

"I think it's about you, about the dad you never knew and the mom you couldn't count on. I think you're trying to protect our sons from the kind of hurt you suffered as a little girl."

"Well, and why shouldn't I want to protect them from being hurt like that?"

"Of course you should. I get it. But are you afraid I would do that to them? *Not* be there when they needed me?"

Now she felt like crying. "No, Easton. Honestly, no. I trust you. To be there for them."

"Good." His eyes held hers. "Do you trust me to be there for *you*?"

"Yes." He was a trustworthy person. She knew it, believed it.

Yet somehow, that *yes* tasted bitter, like a flat-out lie.

He wrapped an arm around her. She wanted to lean into him, to give herself over to his hold on her heart. But she just couldn't do it. Her feelings for him kept growing stronger and that scared her, made her feel out of balance and out of control.

What if it didn't work out in the end for them? What if he realized she wasn't the one for him and he broke it off? She'd never before let a man get this close. If he left, how would she bear the loss?

Sometimes, this bond she felt with him seemed strong, indestructible. And sometimes—like now—it felt like standing blindfolded on the edge of a cliff, her arms stretched out wide and a freezing wind at her back.

His gaze scanned her face as though seeking a point of entry. "We're good, then?"

"Yeah."

He gathered her closer. She let her body relax in his hold. When he tipped up her chin and kissed her, she kissed him back eagerly.

Later, in her bed, she cuddled in close to him. He pulled the covers up nice and cozy. She fell asleep with his warm arms around her.

In the morning, they shared a quick breakfast, the two of them and the boys, before Easton headed off to get ready for work and Payton drove Penn and Bailey to day care.

That night, Easton showed up for dinner. After the kids were in bed, he said he wanted to help with getting them to day care. "Picking them up midday is problematic for me, workwise, but for right now I'm thinking I could get them there in the mornings."

She put on a stern voice. "I know what you're up to. You want to see the facility and meet their day care teacher."

"Yes, I do."

And then she grinned. "Great idea."

Tuesday morning, he followed her and the boys to Heartwood Kidcare. She introduced him to the owner and they filled out a form giving him permission to pick up the boys in case he might need to do that in the future. He met the boys' teacher and got a tour of their classroom. The boys led him around, showing him their cubbies and the class Christmas tree. They proudly pointed out the decorations each of them had made by hand.

That night, he seemed quiet. She asked him what was wrong, and he said, "Not a thing."

She didn't really believe him. But then he kissed her and she forgot her doubts and worries about being left behind, about loving and losing.

There was only how good it felt when he held her, naked in his arms.

The week sped by. He stayed at the farm every night and the four of them had breakfast together every morning. It felt so natural, like any other family, sharing a home, having their meals together.

Saturday night, he took her to the house on the river. He had the table set with nice dishes and a centerpiece of floating candles. Outside, it was snowing, even sticking a little, the white flakes so pretty, caught and spun around by the swirling wind in the glow of the deck lights. They ate roast chicken with new potatoes, and he served her chocolate cream pie for dessert.

She was halfway through her slice of pie when he pushed back his chair and reached for her hand.

"Come up here." He pulled her out of her chair and into his arms. When his mouth covered hers, she sighed in pleasure at the contact. "You taste good," he whispered against her parted lips.

"It's a great pie…"

He kissed her again, even deeper than the first time.

And then he sank to a knee before her. As she gazed down at him, disbelieving, he reached in his pocket and pulled out a beautiful ring, an oval-shaped diamond haloed with pink diamonds in an antique gold setting, channel-set stones glittering along the band. She wanted to burst into tears and yet her eyes were dry, her heart aching.

"I love you, Payton," he said, gazing up at her like she was everything he'd ever dreamed of. "You're the one for me. I want you. Forever. You and the boys are my whole world. I know we have a lot to work out—with your life here and mine in Washington, with the crap my mom pulled and the doubts you have that are so hard to let go of. I don't expect you to marry me tomorrow. But I believe we can do it. We can take our time, figure it out, together. Right now, I just need to know that you love me, too. That you're willing to wear my ring, and someday, to walk down the aisle to me."

She put her hand to her throat. "Oh, Easton, I..." She what? There were no words.

He brushed his mouth across the back of her hand. "Look. I get that it's hard for you, to believe in me, in us. I get that you hesitate. You're afraid it won't work out. But make this start with me. Take this step with me. Say yes to me tonight. Say yes to our future. To the life we can make, together, to the happiness we can share."

Outside, the snow swirled wildly in the wind while inside, there was silence.

He waited, down on one knee, staring up at her, everything she wanted and yet somehow felt powerless to claim.

"I'm so scared," she whispered.

"I know. It's okay. I need *you* to know that I want this, Payton. I need you to know I'm not going anywhere."

The tears rose then. They tightened her throat, blurred her vision. She blinked them back. "I never planned to get married."

"You never planned to have kids, either. But look. Twin sons."

"Yes. You're right, I just…"

He prompted so gently, "What I'm saying is, plans change."

Why couldn't he see? Why didn't he understand? She wasn't up for this. She had no idea how to do this. "I'm just having a little trouble accepting the getting-married kind of change."

"Payton. Are you telling me no?"

"I…" What word came next? It wasn't a yes.

He put the ring back in his pocket and slowly rose. "What do you want now?" he asked much too quietly.

"I, um…"

He took her by the shoulders and looked her squarely in the eye. "I'll say it again. I love you. And this is crap, what you're doing. I think you know that it is. I don't know any more ways to show you that I'm here. That I'm with you. That I want to *be* with you for a lifetime, that you're the one for me."

"And I want to be with *you*. I swear I do."

His big hands moved until he clasped her upper arms. "You want to be with me, but you're terrified that if you say yes to me, I'll suddenly become someone else—and leave you?"

A small whimper of sound escaped her as slowly, she nodded.

His gaze never wavered. "You have to know that makes no sense. You have to know that's just the little girl you used to be talking, the scared little girl who never met her dad and couldn't trust her mother, the little girl who made you walk away from me five years ago."

She gasped. "I didn't… No. We agreed, we said—"

"Stop it." His fingers dug in a little. He didn't actually shake her, but it was close. "You were there. You know exactly what happened. I begged you at the end, just to give me a number. You wouldn't. And we lost five years. I can get past that. I can live with that. I know it was as much me as it was you back then. But you need to stop doing that. You need to give that shit up and let it happen with us, let it be real. You need to trust me and give me a damn chance to trust you back."

"It's just I— We're not ready."

"Speak for yourself."

"My aunt raised me. I need to be here for her as the years go by. My sister's on her own and pregnant. She wanted a baby and there was no special man in her life. You might have noticed that there isn't any man around for her now."

"What are you telling me?"

"I'm saying that I supported her when she went to a sperm bank to get pregnant."

He looked vaguely stunned. "I had no idea…"

"Well, now you do. When she made the decision to be a single mom, I promised her that I would be here for her, the same as she's always been here for me, for the boys. I can't just leave her. I can't just move away—and there's not only Auntie M and Josie to consider. We have to face the hard fact that your mother hates me…"

"No, she doesn't. She'll come around."

"You keep saying that."

"Because I know that she will."

"No, you don't. Not for sure."

"I'll tell you what I know, Payton. You're using your aunt and your sister and my mother as excuses. Excuses not to put yourself out there, not to put your hand in mine. Everything is workable if you'll only take the leap, show a little faith. My mother just needs time to get over herself. And she will."

"It's not only…"

He put a finger to her lips. "Not finished."

She sucked in a hard breath. "What?"

"As for your sister and your aunt, we can hire a good hand to help out around the farm and you can fly down here anytime either of them needs you. You can come back to Heartwood for weeks in the summer, hang out here in the fall. Spend every holiday here—and the boys and I will spend them with you. Probably my mom and dad and Weston, too. I think they will love it here. My dad already does. Whatever you need, that's what I'm offering. Seattle's not that far away. And frankly, I've got the money to pay for the flights to get you back and forth with very little hassle—*we'll* have the money as soon as we're married, because what's mine will also be yours."

"It sounds so good. Perfect. But I just have a little trouble believing in the whole happily-ever-after fantasy. In my experience, life doesn't really work that way."

He stared down at her, shaking his head. "I don't know how to get through to you. I waited for you for five damn years and I have a very strong feeling that the whole time, you were waiting for me, too—your little detour with Kyle Huckston to the contrary. We are a family. You, me and the boys. We just need to start living what we already are."

She stared up at him, longing to believe him. And yet…

"Say something," he pleaded.

"I don't know how to do that, to be what you want me to be…"

"Yeah, you do."

"Oh, Easton. I'm sorry. I just can't."

He stared at her for the longest time.

Finally, he shrugged. "Get your purse and put on your coat." He spoke without inflection. "I'll take you home."

The ride to the farm felt endless. Neither of them spoke.

When Easton pulled up in front of her cottage, he jumped right out, ran around to her side and pulled open her door. "Good night, Payton."

She had a thousand things to say to him. But she knew if she started talking, she would only blubber like a baby.

"Good night, Easton." She swung her feet to the ground and started walking. He drove away as she was letting herself in the front door.

The next day, Easton took the boys out for the afternoon. He dropped them off around four and said he would be there in the morning to take them to day care.

And he was. He took the boys to Kidcare and came by after dinner to hang out with Penn and Bailey until they went to bed. Then he left.

Tuesday night, after he tucked the boys in, Payton couldn't bear the emotional distance from him a moment longer. She asked to speak with him.

"You have anything new to say to me?" His voice was gentle, his eyes kind—and sad.

She stared up at him, trying to gather her courage. Finally, she forced the words out. "I, um, I do love you, Easton. So much. I'm *in* love with you."

"Yeah?" He almost smiled.

"Yeah. And I don't want to lose you. And, oh, I miss you. I miss you so much. And I'm willing to say I'll marry you, to give being engaged a try, for you."

He had that look, the one she loved the best. A look of hunger and hopefulness. "You're willing to give being engaged to me a try..."

"Yes."

He tipped up her chin. That slight touch sent arrows of heat zipping all through her. "I love you, too." He kissed her, quick and hard—and before she could fling herself against him and drag him to her bedroom, he stepped back. "But no. That's not enough."

Her mouth dropped open.

"I'll pick the boys up in the morning for day care," he said. Grabbing his coat off the hook by the door, he left.

"Okay. What's going on?" Josie demanded. "What went wrong between you and Easton?"

It was after nine on Wednesday morning. Easton had appeared right on time an hour and a half before, picked up Bailey and Penn, and headed for Heartwood Kidcare.

Payton poured water over a peppermint tea bag and carried the full mug to the table. "Here's your tea. And you know I should be working on my book right now. Also, I need to get with my assistant." Mandy, her mostly virtual assistant, lived in Florida and shepherded all of her PR efforts. "Zoom call in an hour."

Josie, in an ancient pair of overalls and a waffle-weave Henley, shoved her riot of spiral curls away from her face and rubbed the hard balloon of her belly. "Stop whining. Sit down. Talk to me."

Payton dropped into the next chair over. "He asked me to marry him."

"How horrible."

"Don't make fun of me."

"Talk."

For the next ten minutes or so, Payton told Josie all about Easton's proposal Saturday night. The tears started falling midway through her story, when she got to the part about how she had to tell him no. About then, Tink, snoozing on the floor a few feet from Josie's chair, lifted her head and let out a whine of doggy sympathy.

Josie turned around, grabbed the tissues from the kitchen island and plunked them between them. "Get over here." Payton scooted her chair right up next to her sister's and leaned her head on

Josie's shoulder. Josie stroked her hair and rubbed her back. "Continue."

Payton told the rest, ending with, "All that to say, since Saturday night, he hardly talks to me. Last night, I finally agreed to give being engaged to him a try. He said he loved me, but my offer wasn't good enough and then he walked out the door."

Josie gave Payton's shoulder a nice, firm squeeze. Then she picked up her tea and sipped, after which she put the mug down and resumed stroking her big stomach. "Let's talk about how you can't leave me."

Payton scooted her chair back to where she'd started. "I don't like your tone of voice."

"And I don't like being an excuse for you *not* to marry the man that you love. You're wrong— Easton's right. I will be fine here when you move to Seattle. So will Auntie M, for that matter. Yes, I'll need another hand around here and you two can pay for that. You'll be here for the baby's birth and any other time I need you. How do I know that? Because there are phones and the internet and modes of transportation. Problem solved. To-night, you can tell that man you love him more than life and you can't wait to be his wife. And that means no more being a wussy-pants. No more of…" Josie put on a wimpy voice. "'For you, Easton I'm willing to *try* being engaged…'"

Payton gave her sister the side-eye. "You don't want to get married, either."

"No, I don't. Nor do I have what you have, a wonderful man I love to distraction who would do anything for me and also happens to be the father of my children." On the table, Josie's phone bleated. She picked it up and opened it with her thumbprint. "I'm on call as usual." The veterinary clinic she worked for part-time sent her out to visit local farms and various pet owners a couple of times a day. "Gotta go."

"Thanks for the hug."

"It's what sisters are for."

Payton couldn't help pouting a little. "Even if you are being too hard on me…"

With a grunt at the effort, Josie pushed back her chair. Tinkerbell took her cue from her mistress. She got up and stretched.

"Don't use me as one of your excuses," Josie instructed. "And please don't drive the man you love away. Talk to him. Tell him everything—the icky details about Mom and how much it hurt never knowing your dad. Let him hold you and promise you the world. Listen to him. Believe that he means every word. And when you've done all that, give him something."

"Like what?"

Josie flipped back her enormous head of hair

again. "Something you took away from him, something you were afraid to give him before."

"I have no idea what you're even talking about."

"Get up here." Josie held down her hand. "Give me another hug. Then Tink and I will leave you to your soul-searching and your virtual PR meeting."

That night, Payton almost caught Easton before he went out the door. She almost begged him to marry her, after all, to please just give her one more chance.

But before she could figure out the right words to say, he was gone. She lay wide-awake half the night, rehearsing and rejecting how she might convince him that she loved him with her whole slightly battered heart and was finally ready to make her home with him in Seattle, ready to be his wife.

Thursday morning, the day before Christmas Eve, there he was, on time as always. The boys ran out and jumped in his fancy BMW SUV and off they went.

Payton dragged herself to her desk and tried to work, though mostly she stared out the window at the tangled bare canes of the wild rose bushes flanking her front steps. Beyond the dormant roses, a blanket of sparkling white snow covered the grass between the houses. Three snowmen with carrot noses, charcoal-briquette eyes and smiles made from curving rows of pebbles stood proudly midway between Payton's cottage and Auntie M's house. The snowmen wore old knit hats in red, green and yellow and had sticks for arms. Ernesto had helped the boys make them the afternoon before. Beyond the row of snowmen, Auntie M's house had a tree in the front window. It glowed with hundreds of multicolored lights. More strings of blinking lights lined the door and the eaves. The roof had a glittery mantle of snow.

After an hour spent mostly staring at the pretty winter scene outside her window, thinking of her children and the man she loved and all the things she needed to tell him, Payton blinked hard and focused on her laptop.

"Work. Now," she instructed herself out loud.

But before she'd managed to type a single word, her cell rang.

It was an unknown number, no spam alert. She should just let it go to voice mail.

Something made her accept the call. "Hello?"

"Ahem. Hello? Is this Payton?" A woman's voice, vaguely familiar.

But one she couldn't quite place. "Yes, this is Payton. Who's this?"

"I…" Clearly anxious, the woman on the other end of the call hesitated.

Payton prompted, "Yes?"

"Payton, it's Joyce. Joyce Wright."

## Chapter Twelve

"Joyce," said Payton cautiously. "How are you?"

"Very nervous," Easton's mother replied. Nervously. Payton almost chuckled. "Myron gave me your number. He said you wouldn't mind."

"Of course not. It's fine."

"Payton, I would like to stop by. I would be very grateful to you if we might talk a little, just you and me."

Payton felt a certain lightness in her chest as hope for peace with the grandmother of her children bloomed within her. "All right. When should I expect you?"

"How about now?"

"You're in Heartwood, then?"

"Just down the road, actually."

Payton glanced at the blinking cursor on her laptop. Today didn't promise to be very productive, anyway, writing-wise. "Sure. You have the address?"

"I do."

"All right. See you soon, then."

Soon turned out to be two minutes later, when a giant RV motor home pulling a gorgeous black Jeep Wrangler Rubicon rolled in front of her office area window, thoroughly blocking her view of her aunt's house. The RV stopped.

Joyce Wright, in a heavy winter jacket, jeans and lace-up winter boots, got out. The RV started up again and drove on, following the circular drive past Josie's place and Auntie M's. Finally, the big vehicle sailed away down the access road it had come in on.

Once the motor home was out of sight, Joyce turned toward Payton's house. Her hands in her pockets, the red pom on the top of her wool hat bouncing, she mounted the front steps.

Payton pulled the door open before Joyce could ring the bell. "Hello, Joyce. Come on in."

With a bounce of her red pom, Joyce stepped over the threshold. Payton shut the door as Joyce reached up and pulled off her hat. She looked... sheepish. Possibly even ashamed.

"Thank you, Payton," Easton's mother said, "for not shutting the door in my face."

"You're welcome. Coffee? Something stronger?"

"Don't tempt me. I need a clear head."

"Coffee, then."

"That would be lovely."

Payton gestured at the coat rack on the wall by

the door. "Just hang your coat and hat on one of the pegs and have a seat at the table."

Five minutes later, they each had a mug of coffee. Joyce added cream and sweetener to hers. "Your tree is beautiful."

"Thank you. We all pitched in to decorate it— Easton, me and the boys—Myron, too." *That was when Easton used to come to this house to see me as much as to spend time with our sons*, she thought but managed not to say. "Nice motor home, by the way."

"Thank you. Turns out I like it more than I thought I would. Myron adores it and I adore him, so both of us are happy." Joyce sipped her coffee. "Delicious." At Payton's acknowledging nod, she said, "Myron will be back in an hour."

"Great. The boys will be thrilled. He's wonderful with them."

"He's hoping to tell them that he's their grandfather," Joyce said.

"That's the plan. I've been expecting him—I have muffins if you're hungry."

"Just the coffee is perfect." Joyce glanced down at her own hands wrapped around her mug. "I, um, wanted a little time to talk to you alone." A nervous laugh escaped her. "Don't be frightened. I'm not here to make more trouble."

Payton blew out a slow breath. "I'm glad."

"I'm here to say how sorry I am for being a

raving bitch to you when you were a guest in my home last month."

Joyce *had* been a raving bitch. But hearing the sweet-looking older woman call herself that, well, Payton wasn't sure she approved.

At the same time, she refused to deny the truth in Joyce's harsh description of herself. Really, she wasn't sure what to say now, so she kept her mouth shut.

Joyce started to reach out—but then thought better of the action and sipped from her mug again. "There's no excuse for the way I behaved, other than what happened to Weston several years ago."

"I understand. Easton explained it all too me. He said you were really invested, that you truly believed the woman's story. That she took advantage of you, of your great love for your son and your longing for a grandchild."

"I was a fool. And Naomi played me like a fiddle. I became very attached to her and the baby I thought was Weston's. It broke my heart when I learned Weston wasn't the baby's father and Naomi was only looking for a meal ticket. I promised myself I would never get taken like that again. And I didn't. Instead, when you came to tell us that we had twin grandsons, I treated you unforgivably. I made a fool of myself all over again, this time by denying the double blessing of my *real* grandchildren and accusing you of being another Naomi. Not only that, but it's also taken me weeks to get past the pigheaded, wrong conclusion I jumped to and then to work up the courage to come here and ask you to try to forgive me."

Forgive her? How could Payton do anything else? Just the sight of Joyce at the front door, looking so anxious and ashamed, had done it. "I do forgive you. I really do. It was horrible, that night at your house, but I'm past it. I want to let it go and I hope that you will, too."

"Thank you," Joyce replied in a small voice, her eyes cast down. "You're clearly a much better woman than I."

Payton couldn't take any more. "Stop. Look at me."

Joyce glanced up. Tears filled her eyes. Deftly, she swiped them away. "I'm so glad. So relieved. I cannot tell you *how* relieved. I've had this knot in my stomach since that night I drove you away, a knot from knowing I messed everything up, a knot from the certainty that you would never forgive me, a knot from stewing over whether or not I would ever get to meet my grandsons…"

"Joyce. It's over. Stop beating yourself up. You have my forgiveness." Payton gave her a tissue from the box on the table. Joyce dabbed at her eyes and Payton added, "And of course you will meet your grandsons today. When Myron comes back, we can all three go together and pick them up at day care."

That brought a fresh flood of tears. Payton passed the whole box to Joyce.

Sniffling, Joyce whipped out more tissues. "Weston's gotten himself into some difficult situations…"

"So I've heard."

"But Easton's my good boy. He's the one who tries, always, to do the right thing. Sometimes, he misses out, though, while he's trying so hard to get it right. I'm so glad that he's found you, Payton—and no, he hasn't spoken to me since that awful night in November, but Myron has told me all about you, about how wonderful you are. With Easton. With the children. Myron says Easton is deeply in love with you. And I'm so glad that he's finally found the woman who is just right for him."

Payton felt her own eyes welling. "I, um…"

"What? Sweetheart, what's wrong? What did I say?" Joyce reached across the table.

Payton met her halfway. They clasped hands and held on. "It's nothing you said. It's just that I've had some rough times in my life, in my childhood. And now, I'm having some trouble with…" She faltered.

Joyce encouraged, "With what?"

Payton let out a sad little moan. "With accepting Easton's love."

"Oh, honey." Joyce got up without releasing Payton's hand. Payton rose, too. They moved toward each other around the table and then they were hugging. It was the strangest thing, to be hugging Easton's mother.

Really, after that night in November, Payton had doubted she would ever speak to the woman again. Yet here they were, both of them blubbering, holding on to each other like sharing a hug and crying together was the most natural thing in the world.

When the storm of mutual weeping subsided, Payton grabbed the box of tissues again. She passed a few to Joyce and took some for herself. They blew their noses and dried their eyes.

"Whatever has happened between the two of you," Joyce said, "I know you can work it out."

"I hope so. I really don't want to get into specifics, but I am the one with the problem…"

Joyce patted her hand, but said nothing, leaving it to Payton to divulge more—or change the subject.

Payton went for it. "Let's just say I hurt him. I let him down. And now I don't know quite how to make it right again between us."

"Are you asking me for advice?"

Was she? "Joyce, I'll take whatever you've got."

Easton's mom gave her a wobbly grin. "You want the dos or the don'ts?"

"Both."

"Hmm. Just shooting in the dark here, I would have to say, do put your pride aside. Do tell the truth. Say what you feel in her heart. And for heaven's sake, don't be like me. Don't take forever to reach out and make things right between you."

Before she took Joyce and Myron to pick up the boys, Payton called Easton, just to check in. She'd expected to leave him a voice mail, but he answered on the second ring.

"What's up?" he asked, cordial, but distant, too.

Her heart ached anew just hearing his voice. She saw him at least once a day and yet she missed him terribly. "Your mother and father are here."

"What the hell? Did she—"

"All is well," Payton cut him off. "Joyce and I had a really good talk."

"Did she apologize?"

"Yes. Beautifully."

"Are they standing right there?"

"No. They went out to visit Deke and Dotty so that I could call you in private."

"You're sure you're all right?" His honest concern made her want to reach through the phone and grab on to him, to hold him so close, to promise him everything. To beg him to give her one more chance, to swear on her hopes for their future that she wouldn't disappoint him again.

But that wasn't why she'd called. "Don't worry, Easton. Your mother and I are good. Really good. I called because I want to take them with me to Kidcare to pick up the boys. Is that all right with you?"

"Of course. If you're comfortable with that."

"I am. Also, they're hoping to have the big grandma-and-grandpa reveal."

"Today, you mean?"

"Yeah. And I was thinking you would probably want to be here for that."

"I do want to be there—listen, how about this? I need to shuffle some stuff around, but things are winding down here with the holiday weekend coming up. I'll take off early. You pick up the kids and I'll meet you all at your house at two. Tell my mom and dad to wait for the big reveal until I get there."

"All right."

"You sure you're okay with this?" he asked.

His concern for her feelings made her miss their lost closeness more than ever. "Easton, I'm fine. Penn and Bailey will be thrilled to see Myron. And Joyce can't wait to meet them. We'll have hot chocolate with marshmallows just like in a Hallmark movie."

He actually chuckled. "Get out your guitar.

Wow the grands with the boys' impressive repertoire of Christmas tunes."

"Good idea. See you at two."

As she disconnected the call, her phone buzzed with a text from Josie.

I just said hi to Myron and met the infamous Joyce. They were hanging out with the ponies. Do you need rescuing?

Thanks, but no. All is well. Joyce and I have reconciled. I'm taking both of them to pick up the twins and then later, when Easton gets here, we'll tell the boys that Myron and Joyce are their grandparents.

That's good, right?

It's excellent, yes. Thanks for checking on me. Tell Auntie M I'm fine and not to worry.

Josie wrote back,

Text "Help!" if you need me.

Grinning, Payton replied with a thumbs-up and a string of emoji hearts.

Easton arrived right at two, as promised. When he pulled up in front, the boys stopped singing midway through the last chorus of "Rudolf the

Red-Nosed Reindeer." They'd been singing for a good forty-five minutes by then and were ripe for a distraction.

"It's Daddy!" shouted Bailey as Penn jumped up and ran to the door. Bailey got up and followed.

Easton had reached the top step when Penn pulled open the door. "Daddy, your mom and your dad are here!"

"Hey, guys." He scooped one up in either arm and carried them, laughing and squirming, to the sofa, where he tossed them down. They giggled in delight.

Myron and Joyce, who had settled into the matching wing chairs that faced the sofa, rose in unison. "Son," said Myron gruffly. "Good to see you."

"Easton…" Joyce looked like she might cry.

He went straight to his mother and gave her a hug. "How are you, Mom?"

She sniffled a little and patted his big shoulder. "Much better. Now." And then she went on tiptoe and whispered something in his ear.

"It's okay," he said and kissed her cheek. "All is forgiven."

"I'm so glad…"

Over on the sofa, the boys had stilled as they watched the interaction between Easton and Joyce.

"Hey, Dad." Easton hugged his father, too.

Payton put her guitar back in its case. "Easton, we have hot chocolate. Or something stronger if you'd like."

"The cocoa sounds great."

She got him a mugful with miniature marshmallows on top and he joined the boys on the sofa.

"Delicious," he said after a first sip. He set down the mug and asked the boys, "So I see that you already know that Myron and Joyce are my mom and dad."

"Yes," replied Penn as Bailey nodded.

"I'm not sure how much you know about grandmas and grandpas."

"We know what they are," said Bailey. "At Kidcare we read *Llama Llama, Gram and Grandpa*."

"And *How to Babysit a Grandpa*," Penn reminded his twin.

"That's right. I forgot," said Bailey. "But we don't have any. Our grandma died a long time ago."

"We never got to meet her," added Penn. "But Mom says we have Auntie M and that's as good as any grandma, anyway."

Easton shot Payton a look of amusement with a side of tenderness. Longing burned through her. She'd missed those tender glances of his. To the boys, he said, "I have to agree. Auntie M is just like a grandma in every way, and a very good grandma, too—but what I'm wondering is, do you know how to tell if someone's *your* grandma or grandpa?"

Both boys were frowning now. "Well," said Penn. "Doesn't your mom tell you when you have them?"

"Yes, your mom might tell you," Easton replied. "But the truth is, everybody has grandparents. It's like you said a minute ago, Penn. Sometimes, you never get to meet them."

"Because they're dead, you mean?" asked Bailey.

"Well, yes. Your grandparents might be in heaven, like your grandma. Or maybe they live far, far away."

The boys looked slightly dazed by all this new information. Payton kind of wished Easton would get to the point. He still hadn't completely grasped the literal nature of the four-year-old brain. Penn and Bailey didn't do metaphors. They liked their puzzles nice and simple—and they needed adults to cut to the chase.

Payton almost jumped in to help him out. But he seemed so earnest, so determined to get the twins to take the clues he kept dropping, to puzzle it out, so she didn't interrupt.

"Think about it this way," he said. "You know who your grandparents are because they are the moms and dads of *your* mom and dad."

Now, the boys stared at him in total bewilderment.

And Joyce couldn't take it anymore. She jumped

up. "What your dad's trying to tell you is that *I* am your grandma…" She reached out blindly toward Myron, who sat in the chair to her left. He rose and took her hand. "This guy—" she pulled Myron closer and kissed him on the cheek "—this guy is your grandpa."

The boys flat out gaped. Slowly, they turned to each other.

Penn whispered, "We got a grandma."

Bailey gave one slow nod. "And a grandpa, too…"

"Yes, you do." Once again, Joyce was blinking back tears. "And when you boys are ready, your grandpa and I would love to get a hug from you."

The twins thoroughly understood the concept of a hug. They bounced off the sofa and ran to their newly found grandparents.

A little while later, Auntie M called. Ernesto had volunteered to treat them all to his legendary spaghetti Bolognese.

After dinner at Marilyn's, Joyce and Myron came back to Payton's to help put the kids to bed. They asked if they could hook up their motor home to her electricity.

"Of course," she replied. "But it's cold out. Are you sure you'll be comfortable?"

Joyce beamed. "Myron got the deluxe fourseasons package—including an excellent furnace and extra insulation."

"We're planning a trip to Alaska in that motor home. We'll be camping out on the frozen tundra," Myron announced proudly. "And we will be toasty warm. We also have TV and internet, all the comforts of home."

Before they retired to their mansion on wheels, Joyce took Payton aside. "Talk to him." She tipped her blond head at the hot guy across the room. He sat on the sofa with Myron watching Louisiana Tech play Georgia Southern in the New Orleans Bowl. "He loves you, Payton," she whispered. "It's going to work out."

Payton forced a wobbly smile and gave Easton's mom a nod that she could interpret however she liked. Yes, Payton longed to speak to Easton honestly and directly about the future, about how much she loved him, how she'd gotten past all her fears and only wanted to make her life at his side.

Too bad she hardly knew how to begin.

"Stay," Payton said. Joyce and Myron had gone out to their motor home. Upstairs, the boys were sound asleep. "I've got a few things I need to say."

He didn't seem annoyed. In fact, he gave her a crooked smile. But she couldn't read his eyes. "I guess I can't go anywhere with you blocking the door."

Slowly, calmly, trying to give no hint of the yearning in her heart and the churning anxiety in her belly, she spread her arms to the sides and pressed her back firmly against the front door. "I'm not stepping out of the way, so I guess you'll have to hear me out."

He crossed his big arms over his chest. "I'm listening."

She shot a glance up the stairs. This wouldn't be a conversation their boys needed to hear. "Come into my room." As she turned to lead the way, she felt a surge of stark terror that he would grab his coat and go.

But he didn't. He followed her in there.

She shut and locked the door. "Have a seat."

He still had his arms crossed. "I'll stand."

She drew a careful breath. He'd followed her in here. But she still had no clue how to tell him what she wanted, how to let him know she really was ready to make a life with him.

"It's okay," he said gruffly, and dropped his arms to his sides, as though to signal he was ready, too, open to her—that she should take her best shot and he would hear her out.

"There's stuff," she said. "Stuff I need you to know."

"All right…" He said the two words on a rising inflection.

How to begin? She had no clue, so she made

the first confession that popped into her mind. "I never had sex with anyone but you from all those months before I met you at the Heartwood Inn—until now."

"Except Kyle," he corrected.

"Nope. Not even Kyle…"

He blinked. "But you were engaged to Kyle."

"Yeah. Kyle loves the boys and he'd always had a thing for me since that one time we did have sex when I was sixteen. He came around a lot after the boys were born. He helped out. He spent time with them. And we hung out, too, him and me because we were friends. Because I was lonely. He proposed when the boys were a year old and I told him I couldn't, that it wouldn't work. He still came around a lot. The boys weren't quite three when he asked me to marry him the second time. By then, I thought I would never find you again.

"I said yes. He kissed me. I pulled away. It somehow always ended up like that. He would make a move and I would pull back. It never got anywhere near the point of having sex. We weren't right for each other and, over the next couple of months, when I was never in the mood to get intimate with him, he finally faced reality. He saw that it wasn't going to work. We both knew it at that point, so we called it off."

Easton's eyes were softer now. "I didn't, either—have sex with anyone else after our first week together five years ago. I was in love with you when you left me that last night. I've never *not* been in love with you since our time at the inn."

"And you're no good at casual encounters…"

"Correct." He held her gaze. "What else have you got to say to me, Payton?"

"Maybe a little ancient history?"

"I'm listening."

"When I was seven or so, a few years before my mother died, I started asking her where my daddy was. The first couple of times I asked, she just blew me off, told me nothing. But the next time I tried to get information on my father, she was drunk, I think. Or maybe high on something stronger. She said I could just forget about my damn daddy, that he disappeared the day she told him she was going to have a baby, a baby that would turn out to be me. She said that my daddy didn't want me, and I needed to stop asking her about him."

The hurt on Easton's face—the hurt for *her*—almost made her come undone. "Payton…" He reached for her.

She stepped back. "Wait. I just need to tell you the rest, okay?"

He let his arms fall to his sides again. "Yeah. Go ahead."

"She, um, did change her story later, my mom.

She started saying she really didn't know who my father was. But I never forgot what she said the first time she told me. That was branded on my brain.

"She also used to say that I was like her—not like Alex, the ambitious one. Not like Josie, the earth mother. That I would grow up wild and do what I wanted, and no man would ever tie me down. I guess I kind of bought into that, into her idea of me. It made me feel strong and self-sufficient. I was bold and foolish, too. When you came along, I didn't have sense enough to grab you and hold on tight. Even now, since you came back, since you found me—found *us*, I've still been holding on to my mother's idea of me.

"But, Easton, I'm letting that go now. Because I love you and I don't want to live wild. I don't want to be without you. I see now that it wasn't that I was destined to be just like my mother. I was just waiting, that's all—for the *right* man for me. And, Easton, you are that man. There's no one else for me. Just you. Only ever you."

His gaze never wavered. "I'm right here."

"Oh, Easton…"

"I love you, Payton," he said. "I'm not going anywhere. Since that Saturday night, I've just been waiting for you to realize that we belong together." He stuck his hand in his pocket and brought out that beautiful ring. "I've been carrying this around with me constantly, waiting for the right moment."

"Dear God." She cast her eyes heavenward. "Please let this be that moment."

"Give me your hand."

Her fingers shook a little as he slipped the gorgeous thing on. "It's so beautiful, Easton. I love it."

He held out his arms.

With a soft cry, she went into them, sighing at the sheer rightness of having those arms around her. She laid her head against his heart. "I love you. I love you more than I know how to say. I do want a life with you." She tipped her head back to look at him again. "Will you please marry me? Marry me and we'll live in Seattle, the four of us—for most of the year…"

He dropped a kiss on the tip of her nose. "But you'll come back often, with me when I can manage it. Or on your own, you and the boys, whenever you need to."

"One way or another," she said. "I just want to be yours and for you to be mine."

"I am yours. And we will work it out."

She dared a smile and felt it tremble across her lips. "So that's a yes?"

"Oh, yeah. That's a yes."

"I want to get married right away."

"Yes," he said again.

"I'm thinking New Year's. Would you marry me at New Year's, Easton Wright?"

"Yes, I will, Payton Dahl."

Her breath caught at the look in his eyes. "We should celebrate."

He scooped her high against his chest and carried her to the bed, where he made love to her fast and hard and then slow and achingly sweet.

The next day, Weston flew down from Seattle and Alex drove over from Portland. They had Christmas together, Easton's family and Payton's.

On Christmas afternoon, Myron formally gave the boys their ponies.

Bailey got Deke and Penn claimed Dotty. The boys jumped all over Myron when he told them. He held them in his arms, laughing in delight as they hugged him and thanked him and Penn said, "We love you, Grandpa."

"Grandma, come here!" Bailey reached for Joyce, who stood, misty-eyed, a few feet away. "We're having a hug!"

She stepped close for the group hug and Easton whipped out his phone to capture the moment.

The next day, Weston returned to Seattle and Alex left for Portland. Joyce and Myron stayed on.

The Monday before New Year's, Easton and Payton got their marriage license. On Tuesday,

Payton and Josie drove to Portland, where they had lunch with Alex and found the perfect wedding dress—a retro dream, tea length, with long lace sleeves and a birdcage veil. Payton paired it with red cowboy boots.

On New Year's Eve, Weston and Alex returned to Heartwood. Alex stayed at Josie's house. Weston went to the house on the river with the groom.

Before they left for the night, Payton took Easton into her office and shut the door. "I have a present for you." She took a nine-by-twelve manila envelope from the bottom desk drawer.

"What's this?" He started to open it.

She stopped his hand. "Read it later, when you have a little time to yourself."

He kissed her. "You're very mysterious."

"It's just something I wrote for you once upon a time."

He knew then. "The missing journal pages…"

She pulled his mouth down to hers again and kissed him slowly, deeply. "Have a nice night with Weston."

At the river house, the brothers drank good Scotch and reminisced until one in the morning. When they called it a night, Easton went to bed with the packet of torn-out journal pages.

He didn't sleep much. And he was just fine with that.

At 5:00 p.m. on New Year's Day, in the event barn at Wild Rose Farm, Easton married the only woman for him. The word had gone out to friends and neighbors all over the area. The barn was packed.

Auntie M gave the bride away. Payton had two maids of honor, Josie and Alex. Weston stood up as best man. The twins, superspiffy in pint-size tuxedos Payton had found on Etsy, each carried a ring on a red satin pillow—Penn carried Payton's and Bailey had Easton's.

After the simple ceremony, everybody pitched in to stack the chairs against the walls. Music and dancing went on late into the night, though the older folks and the little ones left early. Penn and Bailey spent the night in the motor home with Joyce and Myron.

The bride and groom had Payton's cottage all to themselves. Easton carried her over the threshold and straight to her room, where he removed her red boots and her lacy vintage dress.

To him, she'd always been the most beautiful woman in the world, but never more so than on this first night of a whole new year when he'd finally made her his wife.

"At last," he said, "it's just you and me, alone..."

She got to work removing his jacket and tie, his shirt and his belt. "You've been reading those pages," she whispered in his ear as she cupped her hand over the bulge at his fly.

"You almost killed me with those." He kissed her. "At least I would've died happy. You realize now we're going to have to do every one of those naughty things you wrote about?"

She pretended to pout. "I missed you for five endless years. I had to write down all the stuff I wished I'd done with you."

"I'm glad you did. And I want you to know that even though I was all alone last night, me and my hand had the best time ever."

She gave his shoulder a playful slap. "You're so bad." But then she trailed her soft, cool fingers down the center of him, unzipped his pants and eased those fingers under the waistband of his boxer briefs. Slowly, she wrapped them around his aching erection.

He groaned. "I've got a bunch of condoms in my pants pocket..."

She pushed him down onto the bed. "I had a thought..."

"Yeah?"

Slipping her fingers into his pocket, she pulled out a handful of pouches. "I never did get on the pill. I know I should've. I kept thinking I would get around to it. But it's been a busy time..."

"Yeah?"

"What if I didn't?"

He liked where this was going. "Get back on the pill, you mean?"

She tipped her head to the side, considering. Her bronze-and-brown hair spilled over her silky shoulder, gleaming in the lamp light. He would never get enough of her. The woman for him. Finally, his wife.

"We might have a girl," she said. "Or another boy. I don't really care which." She pushed him all the way over onto his back. Bending close, she pressed her soft lips to the side of his throat and then whispered in his ear, "You up for that, Easton, for another baby?"

A baby.

One he would be there for from the first. He could watch her belly grow, hold her hand while she yelled at him during the birth. He would cradle their newborn in his arms...

"I'm up for it," he said around the lump in his throat.

"Easton. I love you so much," she whispered.

"And I love you. Kiss me, Payton."

She tossed the wad of condoms over her shoulder and lowered her soft mouth to his.

\* \* \* \* \*

*For more great single-parent
holiday romances, try these stories:*

His Baby No Matter What
*By Melissa Senate*

The Cowboy's Christmas Retreat
*By Catherine Mann*

Merry Christmas, Baby!
*by Teri Wilson*

*Available now wherever
Harlequin Special Edition
books and ebooks are sold!*

### #2875 DREAMING OF A CHRISTMAS COWBOY
*Montana Mavericks: The Real Cowboys of Bronco Heights*
by Brenda Harlen
In the Christmas play she wrote and will soon star in, Susanna Henry gets the guy.
In real life, however, all-grown-up Susanna is no closer to hooking up with rancher
Dean Abernathy than she was at seventeen. Until a sudden snowstorm strands
them together overnight in a deserted theater...

### #2876 SLEIGH RIDE WITH THE RANCHER
*Men of the West* • by Stella Bagwell
Sophia Vandale can't deny her attraction to rancher Colt Crawford, but when it
comes to men, trusting her own judgment has only led to heartbreak. Maybe with a
little Christmas magic she'll learn to trust her heart instead?

### #2877 MERRY CHRISTMAS, BABY
*Lovestruck, Vermont* • by Teri Wilson
Every day is Christmas for holiday movie producer Candy Cane. But when she
becomes guardian of her infant cousin, she's determined to rediscover the real
thing. When she ends up snowed in with the local grinch, however, it might take a
Christmas miracle to make the season merry...

### #2878 THEIR TEXAS CHRISTMAS GIFT
*Lockharts Lost & Found* • by Cathy Gillen Thacker
Widow Faith Lockhart Hewitt is getting the ultimate Christmas gift in adopting an
infant boy. But when the baby's father, navy SEAL lieutenant Zach Callahan, shows
up, a marriage of convenience gives Faith a son and a husband! But she's already
lost one husband and her second is about to be deployed. Can raising their son
show them love is the only thing that matters?

### #2879 CHRISTMAS AT THE CHÂTEAU
*Bainbridge House* • by Rochelle Alers
Viola Williamson's lifelong dream to run her own kitchen becomes a reality when
she accepts the responsibility of executive chef at her family's hotel and wedding
venue. What she doesn't anticipate is her attraction to the reclusive caretaker
whose lineage is inexorably linked with the property known as Bainbridge House.

### #2880 MOONLIGHT, MENORAHS AND MISTLETOE
*Holliday, Oregon* • by Wendy Warren
As a new landlord, Dr. Gideon Bowen is more irritating than ingratiating.
Eden Berman should probably consider moving. But in the spirit of the holidays,
Eden offers her friendship instead. As their relationship ignites, it's clear that
Gideon is more mensch than menace. With each night of Hanukkah burning
brighter, can Eden light his way to love?

*In the Christmas play she wrote and will soon star
in, Susanna Henry gets the guy. In real life, however,
all-grown-up Susanna is no closer to hooking up with
hardworking rancher Dean Abernathy than she was
at seventeen. Until a sudden snowstorm strands them
together overnight in a deserted theater...*

*Read on for a sneak peek at
the final book in the Montana Mavericks:
The Real Cowboys of Bronco Heights continuity,
Dreaming of a Christmas Cowboy,
by Brenda Harlen!*

"You're cold," Dean realized, when Susanna drew her
knees up to her chest and wrapped her arms around her
legs, no doubt trying to conserve her own body heat as
she huddled under the blanket draped over her shoulders
like a cape.

"A little," she admitted.

"Come here," he said, patting the space on the floor
beside him.

She hesitated for about half a second before scooting
over, obviously accepting that sharing body heat was the
logical thing to do.

But as she snuggled against him, her head against
his shoulder, her curvy body aligned with his, there was
suddenly more heat coursing through his veins than Dean

had anticipated. And maybe it was the normal reaction for a man in close proximity to an attractive woman, but this was *Susanna*.

He wasn't supposed to be thinking of Susanna as an attractive woman—or a woman at all.

She was a friend.

Almost like a sister.

*But she's not your sister*, a voice in the back of his head reminded him. *So there's absolutely no reason you can't kiss her.*

*Don't do it*, the rational side of his brain pleaded. *Kissing Susanna will change everything.*

*Change is good. Necessary, even.*

When Susanna tipped her head back to look at him, obviously waiting for a response to something she'd said, all he could think about was the fact that her lips were *right there*. That barely a few scant inches separated his mouth from hers.

He only needed to dip his head and he could taste those sweetly curved lips that had tempted him for so long, despite all of his best efforts to pretend it wasn't true.

Not that he had any intention of breaching that distance.

Of course not.

Because this was *Susanna*.

No way would he ever—

Apparently the signals from his brain didn't make it to his mouth, because it was already brushing over hers.

*Don't miss*
Dreaming of a Christmas Cowboy *by Brenda Harlen,*
*available December 2021 wherever*
*Harlequin Special Edition books and ebooks are sold.*

Harlequin.com

## SPECIAL EXCERPT FROM

*Angi Guilardi needs a man for Christmas—at least, according to her mother. Balancing work and her eight-year-old son, she has no time for romance...until Angi runs into Gabriel Carlyle. Temporarily helping at his grandmother's flower shop, Gabriel doesn't plan to stick around, especially after he bumps into Angi, one of his childhood bullies. But with their undeniable chemistry, they're both finding it hard to stay away from each other...*

*Read on for a sneak preview of*
*Mistletoe Season,*
*the next book in* USA TODAY *bestselling author Michelle Major's Carolina Girls series, available October 2021!*

"Who's dating?" Josie, who sat in the front row, leaned forward in her chair.

"No one," Gabe said through clenched teeth.

"Not even a little." Angi offered a patently fake smile. "I'd be thrilled to work with Gabe. I'm sure he'll have lots to offer as far as making this Christmas season in Magnolia the most festive ever."

The words seemed benign enough on the surface, but Gabe knew a challenge when he heard one.

"I have loads of time to devote to this town," he said solemnly, placing a hand over his chest. He glanced down at Josie and her cronies and gave his most winsome smile. "I know it will make my grandma happy."

As expected, the women clucked and cooed over his devotion. Angi looked like she wanted to reach around Malcolm and scratch out Gabe's eyes, and it was strangely satisfying to get under her skin.

"Well, then." Mal grabbed each of their hands and held them above his head like some kind of referee calling a heavyweight boxing match. "We have our new Christmas on the Coast power couple."

*Don't miss*
Mistletoe Season *by Michelle Major,*
*available October 2021 wherever HQN books*
*and ebooks are sold.*

HQNBooks.com